HUNGER ROAD

a Novella of the Irish Famine

Victoria Tester

The years 1845 to 1851 were years called 'The Great Hunger' in Ireland.
The potato crop failed yearly, due to disease.
Three million people, mostly tenant farmers, perished, or disappeared across the seas.

This is the story of a small village in central Ireland,
told in the voice of a young child,
and it is dedicated to St. Brigid,
and to the people of Ireland and her Great Diaspora.

1

I looked through the open door where Padraig O'Coffey lay dying on a straw bed near the west wall of his cottage. As soon as he finished dying he'd jump up and show us he was, like any long-legged O'Coffey man, the best dancer in our village.

His sons had opened a hole in the thatch of the roof for the passage of the old man's spirit, and an early star winked down.

My oldest sister, Roisin Dubh, tore me away from where I spied at the door.

She looked quickly into the cottage for the sight of Liam, Padraig's oldest son.

Inside the dark cottage, gentle Liam, hot-headed Aengus and young Barra watched their father. Even from the cool yard, we felt their burning grief.

When we heard the old man exhale for the last time, we knew that Liam was lighting a precious borrowed candle.

Then, what I dreaded.

Old Brigid began a long wailing keen. Two other old women keened back. Then my sisters wove their own voices into the mourning song.

I did not. That summer, I was nine years old.

The grown women were strangers, part of something old and frightening. My blood jumped in rhythm to their grief, but I quieted it.

Our potato fields stood in glorious, purple bloom.

The next evening the moon was huge, and the ears of the rabbit in the moon pointed upwards.

Our village was gathered outdoors for Padraig O'Coffey's wake, everyone speaking softly, sometimes merrily, of the dead man's virtues. The men smoked little clay pipes I wanted to try to smoke, too, and the men and the women drank whiskey from small clay mugs.

Sometimes the other children and I looked up towards the open doorway of the O'Coffey cottage. Padraig O'Coffey still rested in his humble coffin.

Beside the coffin, a single candle burned. Who could hold their hand longest over the flame?

It was said that until three hundred years ago Padraig O'Coffey had been a lord, and never stingy.

His huge cauldron overflowed with roasted pigs and milk. His enemies' severed heads dangled proudly from the saddles of his horses. Only his wife, a woman whose wild hair flew like a mane, could run faster than his fine horses.

The one day the lord pierced a stag through the throat with his sword.

But it was no stag.

It was a powerful, wandering poet who lived only long enough to curse the lord. His verses covered Padraig's face with horrible black spots and made him grow thin and shiver and weep on the ground.

The verses brought Queen Elizabeth, who stole Padraig's lands, his wife and his finest black horse and gave them to the English Landlord, who made the horse a bed next to his own.

Then the English made laws against Catholics.

They could not buy or lease land. They could not receive land as a gift. They could not inherit land. They could not rent land worth more than thirty shillings a year.

Padraig O'Coffey's descendants had to divide what was left of the land into twelve parts each time the old man died, and that was why the O'Coffeys lived on a single acre they rented from His Lordship.

Now the vast and ancient O'Coffey lands would go to Liam.

Their dream of the land had been handed down that way for centuries.

Roisin Dubh woke cold at nights from her own dream.

Sometimes she whispered it in the dark. My oldest sister wandered in rags over the lonely roads of old Ireland. No one knew her face, or her name.

Roisin Dubh will marry Liam, Old Brigid says. The cold dream of roads would end.

I wish Liam would marry Granya instead.

But my red-haired sister Granya loves Aengus.

Granya has secrets no one knows what they are. She combs my hair without patience, and slips from the house at night when she thinks we are sleeping.

I want to offer up Granya. Granya could meet you, Liam. Climb the wooded hill with you and lay down beside you under the oaks.

The next morning Father Brennan led our somber procession to the cemetery.

Liam, Aengus, Barra and my stern father Conall Mac Cormaic shouldered the coffin. The women of our village keened, and my fourteen year old brother Michael, along with our other young men, played music on goatskin pipes.

Father Brennan was deafened. He spat out holy words as if against the wailing and the wild music.

I plugged my ears against the music, too, but not for the same reason as the priest.

I liked the pipes, but I wanted to be like St. Brendan who stopped his ears with cloth whenever earthly musicians played.

No music from this earth compared to songs a visiting angel once played for the saint.

I take one hand from my ear and place it in Roisin Dubh's as I stare at Father Brennan. My sister knows I don't like the priest.

Let's melt him into a silver harp with our eyes.

The next month, August, I followed Liam and Roisin when they went into the Landlord's stone barn.

Light gilded the golden hay and the stalls.

I hid and watched Liam lead Roisin to a stall where a black filly stood near a white mare, her mother. The filly eyed Roisin as if maybe her hands were branches of sweet apples, and she might want to know what an apple was but was afraid. Roisin looked back at her, awed.

She was a true mare, Liam explained.

The seventh filly born to her mother, with no colts in between. This meant no evil spell had power over her.

There was a tender silence. I licked the inside of my index fingernail so I could feel its sharpness against my tongue, and watched.

"What's her name?"

"The Landlord calls her Queen's Pride. Her sire won many races."

Everyone knew the Landlord loved, as we did, horses more than gold, and gold more than anything except his youngest daughter. It was said she looked like me except she wore blue silk dresses.

Liam strokes between the filly's ears. It reminds him of the silk dress he wants to give my sister, and of the ancient O'Coffey lands. "But I call her Roisin Dubh, little black rose, after you."

My sister goes to pet the filly, then draws back, wary of the watchful mare. Liam nods to reassure her, and she reaches out again, strokes Roisin Dubh.

Liam and Roisin look at each other and their lips tremble.

Maybe I will yell and yell. Pretend a bee has stung my cheek and nothing can ease the pain.

But I don't.

I watch my oldest sister and her Liam go quietly from the barn. I climb out of the straw and run over to the true mare, who knows me. I stroke her. She lifts her hoof so I can admire the secret patch of four-leaved shamrocks that sprouted and grow where her dam dropped her.

Then I run after Roisin Dubh.

The world is so bright I must fight to keep my eyes open as I run after Roisin and Liam who disappear on the back of the now grown true mare through a field of purple blossoming potato plants.

Blinded by the sun, I run smack into our village priest, Father Brennan, his black robes flying in the wind. He looks at me and smiles and I draw back in fear.

I run past him.

When I look back, the priest has become a raven. He casts a shadow that eclipses the sun and darkens the fields.

I awake cold in the straw bed I share with my three sisters.

It is deep night and the only light is the glow of the smoored peat fire. I stare at Roisin Dubh, whose breath smells like milk. She stares back at me, wordless. She knows that I have had a dream about the priest.

It is unlucky. Something bad is coming towards us. It is better to dream of the devil than a priest, Old Brigid likes to say.

Go to sleep, my sister's black eyes answer. Mary's wing and my own will shield thee. She does not believe in anything except her joy. The secret she shares with Liam.

I need a secret of my own.

Tomorrow I vowed I would practice, like St. Brigid, hanging my woolen shawl on sunbeams.

Not long after, there came the soundless morning. The one without birds.

It was September. A peat fire danced on our hearth. We sat around the table our father Conall fashioned from old crates.

Roisin's wide, careful hands set a heaping bowl of creamed potatoes before us. Father, Roisin, Granya, Michael, Little Mary and I leaned towards the steaming bowl, dipping with our wooden spoons.

I had already heard the extraordinary silence, and I was the only one not eating with real pleasure.

But I could not bring myself to say a word. I shoveled potatoes into my mouth and forced myself to swallow.

It was Michael who said it, between bites.

Still eating more than any of us, including our father. Roisin called our brother a changeling because he could never get a full belly.

"The birds have gone away. They're not singing this morning."

Roisin looked up from her spoon, startled.

She looked at our father, who kept his face expressionless.

Stubbornly, he kept eating. It's the quiet pigs that eat the meal. Then I felt the lightning hit my father's body. He stood up with a flash of dark understanding, as if his hands were charred, and went out.

Michael dug his spoon more deeply into the bowl of potatoes. Granya slapped his hand, leaving a red mark Michael admired.

But Roisin was listening to the silence of the birds. My dark sister left us at the table.

Roisin stood near our father Conall, looking out over our field of thriving potato plants.

And at the strange, solitary cloud that approached through the air, not far in the distance.

Granya, Michael, Little Mary and I went out to stand beside them.

"It's a fog coming in," our father said. "I've seen worse."

They stand, wondering, only a little worried. I think of my dream of the priest, and press my fingers over my mouth.

The other villagers come out of their own cottages to gaze at the strange phenomena, too.

Soon all twelve families in our village, along with Old Brigid and Father Brennan and the Schoolteacher, are outside watching the strange, solitary cloud.

"It's a miracle."

"It's a curse."

"Listen," I say. "The cloud is talking."

I could hear an indistinct voice, a man or a woman or a child, rising.

It mumbled, as if a mile away.

As the cloud approached our village, we watched it disperse into a beautiful, shimmering veil.

It stank, and the stench rolled gently over our potato fields.

We covered our mouths and noses.

As the strange white fog rolled across our fields, they rotted with blight.

Those whose fields rotted first lamented loudly. Black dogs howled, too.

Granya, whose stomach is always weak, vomited.

Michael shook his head at her, and Father shouted for her to go back into the cottage, and for me to take Little Mary.

"Una," Granya warns.

But I stared with one blue eye peeping from the barely cracked cottage door as the fog moved over our father's potato field, ruining it with blight.

As the white fog rolled away from the village, Father rushed to his field. Roisin ran after him, watching as he dug up a plant with his bare hands. The potatoes on the end of the black stalk were tiny, but not yet rotten.

He held the plant high, showing it to us all as if it were lumps of gold.

Roisin began to unearth potatoes with her strong hands.

Neighbors raced into their own fields.

Granya, Michael, Little Mary and I ran from the cottage to help Father and Roisin tear away the rotten stalks. Then we dug up the potatoes with sticks and set them in baskets. It was a stingy harvest, but it was a harvest.

That afternoon Father and Michael dug a pit to store the harvested potatoes to protect them from damp and from the coming winter. The empty dark hole frightened me. I felt better when they poured the baskets of tiny potatoes into the pit, and covered them with earth.

Rain began to fall. The men of our village finished their work and disappeared into their cottages.

We went indoors, to our own fire. Roisin looked pale and worried.

I closed my eyes and tried to see my mother's face, instead. They say there are magical machines. Black boxes that show us, on glass worlds, the faces of those we love and even those long dead. No one I knew had ever seen one of those black boxes.

I had never been in the Landlord's house, but I'd heard the rooms were full of objects called mirrors that showed you yourself as if you had jumped out of your body.

Whenever anyone in the house died, the mirrors were covered in black silk so the dead couldn't look back through them.

Sometimes, if you were dusting the mirror's big frame, you might even see the back of a ghost as it walked away.

I wondered if I would see my mother if I looked into a mirror. Maybe someday, I told myself, I would visit the Landlord's house. I hoped for a vision.

If I could see Mother's face just once, I promised St. Brigid, I would become the bravest girl in Ireland. I would find a way to hang my shawl on sunbeams even on the cloudiest days.

If a man asked to marry me, I would not be foolish like my sisters. I would dangle my eyes onto my cheeks and smile at my life.

But St. Brigid wasn't listening.

Our lonely, hidden village was pelted by rain.

2

Soon after that I began to spy on Father Brennan. There were not many priests in Ireland, and we were lucky to have him, even if we shared the holy man with all of the nearby villages.

Everyone knew he had been hidden in a cupboard during the time of King Henry VIII, and was later smuggled, wearing a devout Catholic princess's finery, into a boat that was guided by seals to Ireland.

Every time Cromwell's soldiers pierced the heart of the priest to an oak tree, they found he gave them a deer's heart instead and escaped by St. Padraig's prayer which made him invisible. He risked his head to hold mass at large, solitary rocks so that Ireland could hold communion with the Holy Spirit of God.

He was branded on the face and castrated and executed many times, but for two hundred years he refused to sell his fine horse to a Protestant for five pounds. He leapt on the horse and rode to France, where they entrusted him with ships and soldiers to run the English out of Ireland.

But the English captured the French ships and the soldiers and sank them to the bottom of the sea, and poor Father Brennan returned to Ireland without even the horse he rode away across the waves.

Now that we were Emancipated, the priest spoke against violent ways.

He carried a potato in his pocket to ward off his rheumatism.

He wrote letters in English with a swan's quill on paper too heavy for the wind to carry. No one knew what the letters said, or how they reached their destinations.

We could only guess where he found the swan's quill.

The Landlord's youngest daughter loved the flight of wild swans. Anyone who killed a swan would be forced to leave the barony, or else be hung from an oak tree.

I crept into Father Brennan's sparsely furnished room. I don't know if it was because I was hungry, or if I felt that since the priest invaded my dreams I had a right to know his secrets.

I stuck a piece of potato peel I found uneaten on his plate quietly into my mouth.

Father Brennan was rubbing the feather of his writing quill against his nose, back and forth, as he formed the words of his letter in his mind and spoke them aloud.

Tonight, he was penning a worried letter to someone he called Your Honors.

"Scarcely a potato," he scratched elegantly, "has gone untouched by disease, and the people are suffering this scarcity of their only food. The tenants, bound to pay rents that take all they can spare beyond a mere subsistence, cannot afford to buy other sustenance."

The bones of the priest's face looked like a church on fire. He wanted Your Honors to listen.

"They will be forced," he scratched, "to eat their seed pota-toes, and will have none to plant in the spring."

He was speaking, I realized, to Your Honors about my village.

I froze, the stolen potato peel caught in my throat, and waited for him to finish.

"I fear," he scratched, "there will be many deaths, unless immediate relief is afforded them."

The priest turned and almost saw me, and then mistook me for the Holy Spirit, or else a mischievous wind.

His candle had blown out.

I'd raced from his room, not even closing the wooden doors of the Church behind me.

Little Mary stayed indoors with me on Samhain.

It was not fair.

We wanted to climb the hill to the festival fire and look out at the fires burning on hills across Ireland.

We could not. Roisin scolded that maybe the fairies would spirit me away again, or I'd see the ghosts of the dead walking around, kissing and dancing. Maybe I would steal another clay pipe and try to smoke it.

She and Granya and Michael turned their clothes inside out and went their way, and Father, carrying a little salt in his pocket, went his.

My sisters were going to meet their lovers, our brother went heaven knows where, and Father wanted to drink whiskey alone.

So by ourselves we dug a small hole beside the hearth and poured milk from Brigid's cow in it, and a small potato for the ghost of our mother, who might visit.

Little Mary and I would welcome her ghost.

Our pig, Gentleman, watched us from his pen against the wall. He grunted for affection. He was hungry and he wanted to eat the food we'd poured into the hole for Mother's ghost.

In the morning we would fill the hole with earth.

"The People of the Otherworld are coming tonight," I told my sister.

"They are going to blight everything green with their breath, and tomorrow everything will look brown and dead."

Little Mary laughed.

I remembered what Old Brigid had told me, too. "The earth is a very old woman tonight. Like Old Brigid. A wrinkled hag. But soon she will be kissed by a young man and will become young and beautiful again."

On the hill, on hills across my country, everyone was drinking and dancing. I could hear their laughter in my head long after Little Mary and I fell asleep, braided into each other.

Morning, we were disappointed. The milk and the potato in the hole looked untouched.

If our mother's ghost had visited us, she had not been hungry.

Our father sat on his stool, his pet crow on his shoulder, staring at the pictures in the flames of the hearth.

Roisin was peeling a bowl of meager potatoes, and Granya was combing her long, twisting red hair. Little Mary was playing with three pebbles Old Brigid had pressed into her hand. Michael was trying to teach Gentleman the little bit of English he had coaxed from the Schoolteacher.

I sat in front of the fire, plugging my ears, listening to a strange music.

Whatever the fire had told our father, it made him furious. I could hear him clearly, even with my fingers in my ears.

"One of you wide awake and dreaming --"

That was me.

"One of you sulking --"

That was Roisin.

"One who killed her own mother --"

That was Little Mary, born after Mother died, Old Brigid said. The baby girl pushed herself out to the light feet first, with only the help of St. Brigid, who our mother had called to save her daughter.

"– and one whoring!"

He was looking at Granya.

"I don't know which is worst in a woman!"

Granya looks as if she will tell Father which sin is worst in a man, then she keeps quiet. Roisin also presses her own lips together.

Father's crow flies over and lands on Gentleman, who welcomes him with a grunt.

Father approves of the pig. The Gentleman will pay the rent when the time comes.

"I will send my chickens to the hill with Una," Roisin says.

I nod. I'll climb the hill with the chickens like I did last year to hide them from the Rent Collector.

Roisin smoors the fire, muttering a prayer.

Little Mary is sleeping. Granya faces the wall, her eyes open, looking into an angry dream.

But I am awake, mouthing the prayer my oldest sister always says before she climbs onto our straw mattress:

I lie down with God and may God lie down with me. Mary's wing at my head. Mary's refuge beneath my feet. Mary's belt around me while I'm sound asleep.

After Roisin is in bed, too, I whisper, "Tell me about when the angel played music for St. Brendan."

Roisin sighs, tired of telling the story. But I know she is not.

"The angel who is named Michael sang and played on a harp of gold for St. Brendan. Music so beautiful that Brendan no longer wanted to stay on this earth."

Why didn't he just go to heaven instead?

My sister knows I want to interrupt, but she goes on:

"Brendan wanted to go straight to heaven. So poor archangel Michael had to stop the music. He put his harp away and would not play anymore, though Brendan begged him to."

I thought the archangel was unfair. If I saw him I would tell him so.

"After that, Brendan always stuffed cloth in his ears when he heard earthly music. Not to be rude --"

It was rude to plug your ears to hear heavenly music when those on this earth were trying to be heard. Everyone told me so. Especially Father Brennan.

"– not to be rude," my sister went on, "but earthly music made him sad. Because nothing could ever compare to the music the angel had made."

I lay awake in the blackness as long as I could with the angel Michael's golden harp burning like a sun behind my eyes.

Our village did its best to outwit the Rent Collector. Neighbors sent their sons with their pigs led by ropes up the wooded hill.

Those who stayed behind in their cottages scattered the tracks of the boys and the animals with their brooms.

Stubborn cows were led out of cottages, children switching at their hindquarters with soft vines.

Little Mary, with the smallest children, swept away the cow tracks with her hands. Cows ambled up the wooded hill.

I knew old men were burying their single, precious coins under the hearthstones of their cottages.

Old Brigid, our village storyteller, sent her cow up the hill with Michael, then went into her yard to face the sun and pray a welcome to the morning.

Brigid and I prayed together, our faces east, the way she taught me.

Then I scrambled up the hillside with Roisin's flock of chickens.

I was high on the wooded hill, but I knew when the Rent Collector arrived on horseback, accompanied by a man driving a cart to load our animals.

Gentleman went wild with fear even before the Rent Collector knocked on the door. Roisin was grim. Granya in tears.

Roisin looped a rope around Gentleman's neck and he grew wilder, struggling harder. Little Mary cried in compassion for him.

I cried, too, as I thought of it in my hiding place above the village.

I knew my father who had been sitting outside the door smoking his pipe would go into the cottage and speak gently to Gentleman, who would quiet a little.

The crow on Father's shoulder would sense human trickery.

Scold my sisters and even my brother who was off somewhere hiding with Old Brigid's cow.

I felt the dark wind from the crow's wings as he flew out the open door.

I huddle against a large oak, the chickens flocked at my legs. A chicken jumps into my lap and I stroke it.

"You chickens are all Vikings," I whisper. "The Vikings brought you to our country with the foxes."

The word "fox" scares the fat chickens, but not me. I love the red flash of foxes, even if they were the ancient dogs of the Vikings.

The Viking chickens do not like us, they say in our village.

That is why they scratch near our hearths, trying to set our houses on fire.

At night they dream of sailing home to their Viking country, but every morning they forget they were going to go home.

I scold the chickens for their forgetfulness. "Now I have to hide you from the Rent Collector."

After that came a hungry winter.

Our village was draped in white snow, darkened only by the blue smoke from our peat fires as it trailed upwards from the roofholes of our cottages.

There was almost no talk, no music.

You rarely saw a soul moving around in the strange cold.

Even Old Brigid kept to her own fire, and kept her stories to herself.

If it were not for the birds, ours would have been a silent world.

January, we sat around the table with our father Conall, dipping our wooden spoons into a small, shared bowl of potatoes.

We finished the bowl, no one too proud, not even Granya, to suck the wood of their empty spoons.

Only one chicken pecked near the hearth now, trying to set our cottage on fire.

No one spoke.

Father stared at the fire and grew furious.

Little Mary's dimples disappeared, and I knew my eyes were big as an owl's, bigger than they had ever been, because of how much larger everything had grown.

This made Father angry with Roisin and Granya and Michael.

I closed my huge eyes when he growled, "We will only come to this table every other day, so that Una and Little Mary may eat everyday."

Roisin nods, but she is so pale I am afraid her thin face will crack like a plate. Granya nods, too. Michael makes a bitter sound. Then Granya starts to cry, quietly, and everyone ignores her except Little Mary, who starts to cry, too.

I go to the straw bed where I sleep with my sisters.

It smells like sweat and milk and something sharp, maybe a hard apple, which I know is Granya's anger.

There is something else.

I lift the mattress and find it: a silk dress, glistening like wet shamrocks. My mouth falls open in wonder.

I hold it up for everyone to look at.

"Look. It matches Granya's eyes."

She flushes. Roisin looks frightened. Our father Conall Mac Cormaic glares at Granya. "You're no daughter of mine."

Granya is mute. Stubborn and ashamed.

She looks as if she will bolt out into the harsh winter, wearing the green silk dress she's kept hidden under the straw of our mattress.

It is my fault.

Her bare feet will turn red in the snow.

Maybe her feet will turn black and fall off.

Roisin sees this, too. My dark oldest sister knows about wandering lonely roads. "Let her sell it in the spring. When our hunger is worse."

"We may live after losing our lives, but not after losing our honor."

There is no answering our father.

We are afraid to breathe for the rest of the winter, in case we fan the fire that has become Conall Mac Cormaic.

3

That night Roisin acted like someone I did not know. She held a knife after she thought we were long asleep. Granya woke in pain.

"Have you gone with the fairies?"

"Aengus asked me for some of your pubic hair. For a going away charm to America."

That was what a boy did, I had heard, if he loved a girl and wanted her to keep loving only him when he went away.

Or else the boy would ask her sister for a charm made of his love's menstrual blood.

I felt sorry for my sisters because they had hair between their legs and bled from between there every month.

I hoped it never happened to me.

Granya was annoyed.

"Did you get enough?"

Roisin held the hair up to her own chin.

"He could make himself another red beard with this."

My sisters collapse with laughter they smother under our blanket. I consider Aengus with two red beards, and they don't see my frown in the darkness.

They lay whispering, illumined only by the light of the smoored peat fire. Secretly, I listen.

"If I sell the dress I can use the money to go to America with Aengus."

"What goes far away turns cold."

I imagine Granya trembling with cold on a ship to America. Her lips turn blue. Her hands redden. The ship gets stuck in the ice of a perfectly frozen Atlantic.

Granya wanted to work for Roisin's passage when she got to America, and to send for her, too.

My Roisin Dubh would go far across the water?

Roisin would not hear of it. "Who would we become," she wanted to know, "if we abandon Ireland? Our hope is in the land." She said we would plant again when the spring comes.

Granya told her they were working to free Ireland over there in America. Someday they would come back across the ocean and run the English out.

I saw it.

The Landlord and his wife and children flying through the air away from us, like ducks scattered by the hunter's gun.

I knew the men of our village wanted to put all of their money into one pocket to buy a gun, but I couldn't understand why.

Something told me it had to do with the English.

They did not speak our language and they had come to our country and taken our lands. In the old days we had not paid rent to landlords. We had been the lords.

Now most of us wore no shoes.

"They are dreaming," Roisin says about the men who claim they will return. "They'll never come back."

She was probably right. I had never known anyone except St. Brendan who returned from across the Atlantic.

Then Granya tells Roisin that the silk dress the color of wet shamrocks is stolen. That Aengus stole it from the Landlord's daughter. Granya must go away to sell it. We don't know where.

I fell into a restless sleep of roads Granya walked to sell her dress. I raced behind her. I could not keep up and I could never reach her, except for the long ends of her twisting curls. I'd touch one and she'd whirl around and I'd wonder at how changed my sister was. Because instead of slapping me, she'd offer to cut off the curl, leave it behind with me.

Before I could say no, she'd cut the curl so that it fell into my hand.

I ran behind Granya who was now sheared as a boy, my hands clutching her curls, wanting to give them back to her. But I could not match her long strides.

I woke and slept and woke. I dreamed again.

I walked near the Landlord's stone barn because I wanted to see the true mare that Liam, who cared for the Landlord's horses, called Roisin Dubh. The filly knew I was coming and called out to me.

But as I got closer to the barn I saw eight violent men, sons of Molly McGuire. Their faces were blackened and they were dressed as women.

I thought I saw Aengus and Barra, his younger brother, among the black-faced women. And then I saw the woman who looked like Aengus hold her angry torch to the thatch roof of the Landlord's barn, and I cried out.

Inside the barn, I knew, the true mare was whinnying in terror at the flames.

The spreading fire lit the darkness like a sudden dawn and the Mollies ran away. A hobbling old man and a boy, two of the Landlord's caretakers, came running.

We flung open the barn doors.

Roisin Dubh jumped her stall.

Dashed out, followed by her dam. Ran past us into the green, wet fields. The boy and I looked at the burning barn.

Abandoned it and ran after the horses.

The sun was high when I woke, and my feet, which I rinsed clean before bed every evening, were licked with mud and grass.

It was St. Brigid's Day.

Old Brigid had promised it would come even if she did not live to see it.

Last night we had left a piece of cloth outside the house, and St. Brigid, passing by, had blessed it.

Now it was kept, folded and precious, in our cottage.

Old Brigid was milking her white cow, the cow she had given the most beautiful name in the world: Niamh of the Golden Hair.

She squirted milk into a large clay mug for the twelve of us children who watched, hopeful.

We liked that Old Brigid, and no woman in our village, ever milked her cow silently. The songs they sang as they milked were part of the milk.

The songs went into the milk and then into you when you drank it.

Old Brigid crooned: God bless you cow. May your calf be twice blessed. Come Mary and sit. Come Brigid and milk. Come Archangel Michael and bless the dead. My black cow, my black cow, a like sorrow afflicts you and me.

You grieving for your lonely calf. I, for my beloved son under the sea, stolen. My beloved son under the sea, my heart.

Old Brigid, it was said, and we knew it was true because of her huge breasts, breasts our father said she could throw over her shoulder when she ran, had given birth to one thousand sons. They had scattered away, breaking her huge heart.

The most handsome ones were under the sea, green and drowned, but still handsome.

Others had gone to Dublin, to England, to India, to Africa.

The sons who played violin and who leapt highest had gone to America and to Canada, where it was said they were working to free Ireland.

Someday those sons would return, though Roisin did not believe it, and run the English out.

Others of Brigid's sons had stolen bread or oranges and were now prisoners in Australia, breaking stones to build another country the English could rule.

The rest, we knew, had been taken by the fairies.

Brigid protected them by dressing them in girl's clothes when they were small, but when they grew they put on men's clothes and wandered close to fairy mounds. They had even entered the fairy mounds, hoping to find the gold within the dangerous fairy forts.

The few remaining sons had wandered onto stray sod and it had tricked them into losing their way. Now they wandered, forever lost, not knowing the way home.

We hoped someday the spells on the ancient woman's sons would be lifted.

But Brigid did not seem sad. She rubbed Niamh's udders with dung so the fairies would not steal her milk.

Roisin and Granya, weak in their shawls, watch the old storyteller and rally with the spring.

I pet Niamh of the Golden Hair and lean my ear to her muzzle to see if she tells me a secret. Niamh tells me she is getting old. Old Brigid, she says, is getting old, too.

"That is no secret." I want to know exactly how old. "How old are you, Brigid?" I wait for Granya to pinch my arm.

But I'm lucky. Granya is weak after our long winter. I could yank her long curls and run and she would not chase me.

"Older than the mist," Brigid says. "And older by two."

The mist must be very old. It hides so much. You cannot walk far in it without coming to harm.

They say Old Brigid has hidden all the gold her sons sent her from faraway. She could keep all of our bellies full if she weren't hoarding it.

But I know Brigid hoards no gold. She has only forgotten where it's hidden.

Old Brigid hands the filled mug to Erin, the oldest child among us.

Then she steps into her cottage. I peer in.

A white dog also older than the mist lays by the fire. A small field mouse warms his bones in a corner of the hearth. A freshly woven St. Brigid's cross hangs over Niamh's byre to protect her.

Roisin and Granya follow Brigid inside. The old woman lifts a jug of poteen from a corner and pours some into a wooden mug for my sisters.

They must drink it slowly, drop by drop, because their stomachs have been empty for so long.

At the first drop, my sisters' eyes begin to shine a little.

Little Mary and I go into the cottage with the other children and huddle quietly.

Erin shares the mug of milk among us.

Old Brigid, who loves an audience as much as she loves her solitude, sits in her oddly fancy chair.

It is unlike any chair in our village, even Father Brennan's.

It may be the most beautiful chair in all of Ireland.

It was said that the chair had been sent to her from across the sea, thousands of years ago, by her favorite of her sons.

Some said it came from Scotland, others Wales, and some from Spain.

Others said it came from beneath Ireland herself. That the son had stolen the chair from the fairies, or from the Tuatha de Danaan who lived underground in Ireland.

Its huge wooden back and arms and legs were carved with spiraling tree branches, swans, salmon, deer and foxes, and a smiling naked woman whose hair twisted around her body like a mermaid's tail.

Brigid sat in the chair. The newly kindled fire danced on the clean swept hearth as if it were playing with us. A spark from the new fire leaps into Brigid's eyes, and we know she is going to riddle us.

Make our eyes light with fear we enjoy.

"I see him approach through the fairy ring. The man with no shirt, no belt on him. The man with feet that are hard and thin. Over all that's alive he always will win!"

We huddle, excited, knowing Who it is.

"It is Death!" we shout.

"Death it is," Brigid approves our quick wisdom.

Before we have forgotten Death, she riddles us again.

"I went out at the break of day, and spied what in the grass there lay. Not fish, not meat, not blood nor bone. I kept it until it walked on its own."

We are stumped. Erin whispers: "A rainbow?"

It is not a rainbow.

Little Mary brightens. "Butterfly." It is her first word this spring. She does not know the world has not always been a silent, hungry place.

"A butterfly does not walk, it flies," Erin scolds.

"An egg," I chime. "An egg is what you might find at the break of day."

"An egg it is!" Brigid beams.

And then before we can take another breath:

"What is big as a horse and light as a feather?"

Granya, the poteen waking the tip of her tongue, tries:

"A ship on the sea."

No, not a ship on the sea.

We look at each other.

"A cloud," Erin guesses.

No, not a cloud.

"What is big as a horse and light as a feather?" Roisin sings. "It is the horse's shadow!"

"It is the horse's shadow," everyone cries.

Was that the wind of something big as a horse and dark as a shadow galloping towards us?

I was afraid because my dark sister knew the answer of the horse's shadow.

That shadow worried me. I thought of my dream of the true mare running from fire, and my grass-stained feet.

I stayed close as I could to Roisin for the rest of the spring, until she swore, annoyed, that I had become a second heart stuck up under her ribs.

4

By St. Padraig's Day we planted our few wrinkled seed potatoes into long rows of raised earth, our lazy beds, and fertilized them with pig and cow manure.

Everyone, from Old Brigid down to Little Mary, worked in the planting.

We looked at ourselves and each other, when the work was done, and saw how thin we had become.

We had survived a winter of hunger, the most severe I had known.

Others, I knew, had seen worse.

All winter we had watched the strain of hunger in each other's faces.

Even Roisin Dubh, who was always strong, was now only bones.

Only her dark eyes were huge.

When I looked into them I saw the whole village. Our hope in the harvest to come.

Even the Schoolteacher had grown thin and pale as a ghost. He lived by the gifts of the village, and for months we had nothing to give.

Roisin and the mothers of the other children had gone hungrier than usual so that the teacher might eat a little.

That the Schoolteacher was ragged and his feet as bare as ours only made him more heroic to us.

We knew his golden chestplate was hidden somewhere in the earth among our cottages, and that the cows had trampled that spot so it could not be found.

We told each other he knew the language of cranes and that when our last lesson from the single, dusty book in his possession was finished, he would put away the book and teach us that secret language.

The Schoolteacher was not from faraway, though he had the eyes of a perpetual stranger.

He was born in a humble village near our own, but he had gone faraway, like St. Brendan, to learn many things.

He went to Dublin and to Spain and to Rome, and then he returned to us with the dusty book and a face so changed that only the old people recognized him.

This, they said, was because he was killed and escaped as many times as Father Brennan.

He was our hero, even when he threatened us with switches he tore from birch trees.

He did not look old, but for more than two hundred years he had taught secretly behind hedges and large rocks and ruins: Irish poetry, our history, mathematics and astronomy.

When he was very young he was an accomplished silversmith, and he once broke the law by forging a pike destined, they said, for the head of Queen Elizabeth.

When English soldiers came after him, he escaped into the hedgerows on a horse so beautiful it made a young English woman go blind.

Her husband tried to force the Schoolmaster to sell the horse for five pounds, but instead the Schoolmaster fled with the blinded wife and restored her sight through science and water from a holy well.

The woman went back to her husband when she saw the Schoolmaster was only a poor Catholic scholar.

After that, the Schoolteacher's father had joined the Church of England so that he could by law send his son to Spain to get a Catholic education, and there, or else in Rome, the Schoolmaster had traded the blinding white horse for the dusty book in Latin.

Sometimes we wished he had not.

Today he drilled the thirty children of our village in our lesson.

"Has Ireland any claim to antiquity?" he asked us fiercely.

We were not afraid. We knew the answer.

Together, we told him:

"Yes, her claim to antiquity is better founded than any other nation, except the Jews and the Egyptians. No nation on the face of the globe can boast of such certain and remote antiquity. None can trace instances of such early civilization. None possesses such proof of its origin, lineage or duration of government."

He was a hawk, ready to swoop. "But is not Ireland's ancient history blended with fable?"

"This cannot be denied," we answered, happily. "But the early records of any nation, except those of the Jews, are blended with fable."

By June our potato fields were dark green again, thriving with purple blossoms that were a promise of the harvest to come.

We welcomed the rain that soaked the fields. But the rain, like a too frequent guest, outlasted our welcome. It fell day after day until our fields were so sodden we did not know how they could hold another drop.

Roisin worried that our fields would simply float away. Granya consoled us that our cottage would turn to a boat as well, and follow the field to the sea.

Our father Conall damned the smoke of those new inventions, the locomotives, and the electricity from too many summer storms.

They would be the ruin of the potato crops all over Ireland.

His pet crow flew away from his shoulder and did not return. Maybe it drowned.

I walked out with him in the heart of July into the unstopping rain.

We walked to the edge of our field.

My father is grim. The more rain he sees, the brighter his eyes burn, as if the devil is adding peat to a fire in his head.

I plug my ears. Maybe I will hear heavenly music that will drown out the rain. I bury my toes in the mud like frogs. There is nothing else I can do.

My father scoops a handful of earth from our field and it runs like a brown river from his fingers. He throws what it leaves in his hand down in disgust.

He is afraid for our potato crop. My father Conall is so afraid for our potato crop that his fear stands beside him like a silent, grown man, and most days now there are two Conalls.

We stand there, myself, my father and his fear, under the steady rain.

I flinch when my father reaches out his hand.

But it is gentle on my bright head. It brings tears to my soaked cheeks.

"I want to see my mother's face," I beg.

"Look at the rain, girl," he mutters.

In August, before the first light, we heard the dogs begin to whine and howl.

Alarmed, we rose in confusion in the darkness.

Roisin rekindled the fire with a quick breath.

We tumbled outside and could make out very little.

Then we and our neighbors exclaimed as our noses were hit by the sulfurous stench of rot.

The first light of the sun hit the horizon, illuminating our fields. The thriving plants, now peppered with brown spots, wither and turn black before our eyes.

Our neighbors, standing in their own fields, watch as the blight spreads.

Our father rushes into his field. Barks orders at us.

"Rip off the stalks so the blight won't get to the potatoes! They'll be safe in the ground until harvest!" We race, even Little Mary races, to tear off the withered stalks and throw them out of the lazy beds.

Outside there was the dusk of an early September evening. Little Mary and I each sat before one small potato.

I look up as a face I cannot make out appears in the opened window. My heart stops. I drop my spoon.

"It is the Hunger Man!"

Everyone looks towards the window.

The Hunger Man is an old spirit who travels the roads of Ireland in times of great hunger, begging. He may visit you, looking like a hungry stranger.

If you give him something to eat, he will bring you good luck.

But I am afraid, because he is a spirit and I have only one small potato and so does Little Mary.

Roisin goes to the window. Looks out, sees no one. Granya, twirling a red curl, looks oddly guilty.

"It is only the moon," Roisin comforts us.

But our father is stern. "Leave half of your potato on the doorstep for him."

"We have nothing left to offer an old superstition," Granya answers sharply. I like this about Granya. Her tongue our father Conall says can clip a hedge.

But our father answers that Granya would offer a spirit an egg only if it promised not to break the shell. More than anything else, the fairies hated human selfishness.

Roisin, I can tell, wants to contradict our father, too. Wants to defend my little potato against being divided for a spirit who has already disappeared.

She opens her mouth, then closes it.

Michael, too, is angry inside his closed mouth.

"Tomorrow we will dig up the harvest," our father consoles.

"Let the Hunger Man dig it up," Granya whispers.

I don't want to, but I carry the uneaten half of my potato outside and set it on the step.

I could eat it quickly and maybe no one would notice. Maybe my father hopes I will eat it and not tell anyone.

But I don't. I look around for the Hunger Man.

Maybe he is watching to see if I offer him something.

Our cottage needs good luck. Our village, and all of Ireland needs good luck.

I go back inside and close the door.

That night, Granya rose and went without her shawl into the cold. But the shawl would not have kept her warm because she was also cold with shame.

My sister ate the potato half on the doorstep under the light of a spying moon. I told no one.

The next morning our whole village walked into our fields with bags and baskets.

We went to work among our lazy beds, in hope of at least a meager harvest.

Instead of potatoes, we unearthed blackened masses of corruption.

Potatoes that burst with rot.

We realized, all over Ireland it was realized, that our entire year's food was destroyed.

My father Conall Mac Cormaic stood apart from us all in the middle of his field. Holding out his muddy hands as if they were no longer part of his body.

Michael lay down laughing in the rotten field as if he were gone with the fairies.

Father Brennan raised his hands in angry prayer towards the sky.

The Schoolteacher hid his face in his arms.

Liam, in his own field, fell to his knees and looked wildly towards us, at Roisin Dubh.

Aengus and Barra threw their rotten clumps back against the earth.

Old Brigid began to keen.

Roisin joined in, then Granya. All the women began to keen, wailing loudly in despair.

I began to cry.

Our lamentation rose over the countryside and joined the lamentations of others across our green island.

We knew our end had begun.

5

Right after that, the black box was born in my head.
Roisin Dubh said it was only a fever, and made me lay in our straw mattress.

It was a shabby, odd gentleman in Quaker clothing who carried the box.

He was fat and gentle, and walked into my country with a look that was apologetic.

He walked over a narrow bridge from an English ship onto our green island, escorting the black box.

I knew at once that it was a large magical new invention: the camera.

I heard a man from aboard the ship whisper that the fat gentleman was called the English Photographer.

A porter rushed forward to help with his two carpet bags. I saw they were heavy and maybe they were full of marvelous things.

Beggars mobbed the English Photographer, holding out their hands, tugging at his black cape, throwing blessings on his head.

He was mortified.

Suddenly, he did not want to be in Ireland.

He talked to a woman named Mary in his head.

Mary was back in England, reading his letter, her hand over her growing belly where a baby hid.

My love, the English Photographer told her. You say that to avoid persecution, the Irish poets of long ago hid their love for Ireland in the symbol of the black rose.

But I have promised not to hide from you, in spite of your condition, the things I must see in this country. I will write to you faithfully as I record, through the natural magic of Henry's invention, the suffering of the people here.

Stay strong, Mary, and I will, too, and with God's help we may effect a change in English policy towards Ireland.

The English Photographer swallowed the hidden apple in his throat, and moved forward in the crowd.

He did not see me watching him and the intriguing black box.

If he saw me, he thought I was the shadow of his cape, or the shadow of the box.

He escorted his magic box into the cab of a horsedrawn carriage.

The horse could see me. Horses can see spirits. If you are in a haunted place, look between a horse's ears and you will see the spirits, too.

I stroked his sides and offered him all I had: a handful of long grass.

The porter lifted the two heavy carpetbags high to the roof of the carriage, and accepted a coin. The horse knew it was time to pull the English Photographer and the black box now, and the carriage rolled away.

I saw the gentleman's broad, square face looking out at the starving beggars through the carriage window. He was shaken by his welcome to my country.

He hated himself for his fear, and his self-doubt.

He touched the black box for the strength of its magic.

Then he faltered, and closed the black curtain of the carriage on Ireland.

Roisin smoothed my damp hair and offered me water.

She insisted that I stay, that I open my eyes, but I went back.

I didn't know where I was. It was a large hall in a manor that smelled yellowed as the pages of Schoolteacher's dusty book. Even indoors, I could tell the sun was fallen.

The walls were sad and gray. I smelled evil ghosts, and also the merry ghosts of beautiful Irish women.

The English Photographer sat before a fire in a huge fireplace, with a Landlord who was neither Irish nor English, but both.

The Landlord was drunk because he shot his hounds this morning. The bastards were eating meat that could go to the poor.

He was sorry for the condition he met the English Photographer in. He called the English Photographer John, and he asked how his cousin Mary was.

Sometimes he thought he saw me from the corner of his eye, then he drank more brandy so I would go away.

I stepped closer.

"We are expecting our first child in December," the English Photographer told him, shyly.

The Landlord proposed a toast. He poured more brandy into his own glass, but the Photographer still did not want any of the amber liquid.

I took his glass and touched my tongue to a drop that some-how made its way to the bottom. I watched them as the room swayed.

The Landlord told John that Quaker or no he would send a bottle with him to keep him steady on his trip through Ireland.

"You will need it. You are mad, of course, with your so-called natural magic, but it's a good madness." The Landlord was as intrigued by the black box as I am.

It hovered near the Photographer's shoulder like a black guardian angel.

I could tell the Landlord wanted to hold the sides of the box and look into its glass eyepiece, but he said instead:

"The most transitory of things, a shadow, the most proverbial emblem of all that is fleeting and momentary, may be fettered by the spell of our natural magic, and may be fixed forever in the position which it seemed only destined for a single instant to occupy."

"Henry Talbot is a genius!" The English Photographer was radiant.

"Talbot is a greedy fox," the Landlord answered.

The English Photographer broke himself and a few close friends to afford the patent for the fox's calotype process.

"We have opposite wishes, you and I," the Landlord told him. "You wish to make what should be fleeting forever fixed."

He looked around the great hall at his ancestors' portraits. "I wish to turn what has seemed permanent back to forgotten shadow."

Angry men in stiff, wide collars looked down at us from the walls, and I leaned into the safety of the men's shadows. I know neither is a coward, even if they are Englishmen.

"The time of the Irish landlords must be declared over. This estate is entailed, John. I hold it during my lifetime, but I cannot sell it. I could pass it down to an heir if I weren't too lazy to marry, but then my heir could not sell it either." The Landlord shook his head. Looked towards me as if I were a window to the night. "Penniless, we've been playing at castles for two hundred years. I am tired."

I am tired, I am tired.

But he does not look tired. He looks huge, like he will fight a bull.

"And your tenants?"

The English Photographer wanted to know, his face serious.

"Stuck on a boat like cattle." The Landlord spit into his own glass and tossed the liquid down. "It was cheaper to pay their passage to Canada and lease the land to a stronger farmer."

"The soil here is fertile." John looked at his own empty glass.

I remembered our blighted field and threw the glass to the floor. John apologized.

"Neglected as an ugly virgin," the Landlord said. "It must be made available for sale. If the poor devils can't buy it, they pay rent so high they can't improve their farms."

"But land reform?" John hesitated.

"You are a man of light and religion," the Landlord warned. "But this famine is a matter of earth, and requires an earthly answer."

John was firm in his Quaker suit. "We must believe some good will come of this famine. We cannot question Heaven's Purpose in sending it."

The Landlord shouted so loud his ancestors on the wall trembled and flaked.

But I am not afraid. I like him when he shouts.

"I can and I do, John! That fox's machination will open your eyes."

But my throat closes when he adds: "The people of Ireland are in danger of perishing, utterly, from the face of the earth."

Later that night, the English Photographer was sleepless in a large room in the gray manor. He got out of bed in his nightdress and sat next to the black box.

Then he walked over to the large windows.

Opened heavy shutters onto a full moon.

We heard a whinny in the darkness, and saw the shadows of three horses carrying away their own thieves.

It was the fairies who steal horses and ride them to exhaustion during the night. Shaken, the Photographer went back to the black box and looked through it at the moon.

Then a cloud passed over the moon and I awoke in the straw, sweating into Roisin's warm side.

I recovered from my fever and was playing Blind Man's Buff with the other children of the village. They spun me around three times. The earth tilted, and I went chasing blindly after the sound of stifled laughter.

And ran smack into Father Brennan.

I tore the rag from my eyes.

Before the priest could flog me, I ran to tell the village the priest and Liam had returned. Everyone, even Old Brigid who knew most things without being told, came out to hear the good news.

Father Brennan announced the rumors we heard were true.

The government would build a road. There would be work for the men, down to any boy of sixteen.

Michael said he would add a year to his age so he could work. So did Liam's youngest brother, Barra.

"Pay is not much," Liam told the men. "But it's six pence a day."

"Is there no work for the women?" Roisin asks. All of the women want to know.

Liam shakes his head and the women look at each other in disgust.

"It's twelve miles there, twelve miles back," the men say.

They nod, resigned. "We'll go."

Two hours before the next day's dawn, the men of our village, young to old, walked the long road to the Roadworks, led by Father Brennan.

We heard everything later.

Our men arrived at the Roadworks Headquarters at dawn. Men from neighboring villages were already present.

The Roadworks Authorities sat at a table with a large, official book. Six policemen stood nearby to keep order.

The villagers stood in line to present themselves and to have their names recorded by the Authorities.

Our men reached the Authorities' table.

First in line was my father, quelling the fire in his eyes.

"Name?" the Authority asked.

"Conall Mac Cormaic."

"Are you a tenant in your village?"

"I hold half an acre from his Lordship."

"Then you cannot be hired. Anyone holding more than a quarter an acre is not eligible to work on the road."

"Every crop in our village failed. What good is the half-acre to me now?"

"If you wish to build a road, you'll have to give up your half-acre. We can only hire those men most in need. Return with a paper from His Lordship saying you've given up your holding."

Most men in our village did not speak English. They asked, in Irish, "What is he saying?"

Others explained, "No one holding more than a quarter acre can work."

"The crops are failed," the men replied. "What use is the land now?"

Conall Mac Cormaic spoke bravely and sensibly to the Authority, it was later told. When he returned home, his clothes blackened, he would tell us nothing.

"My family, we have nowhere to go, and what will we live on next year, after the road is built, if I give up my land?"

"Move out of the way now," another Roadworks Authority, with the eyes of a dead salmon, told Conall Mac Cormaic.

"Write my name in your book. Six pence a day!" my father demanded, the fire leaping from his chest. The police guards saw the fire and moved threateningly towards Conall Mac Cormaic, who took no step backwards.

Liam moved forward in the line of men. They asked him his name and if he held land and he told them that by tomorrow he would not. He told them he would bring them the paper from the Landlord tomorrow.

"Write down my name: Liam O'Coffey."

Father Brennan pledged the Authorities his word that Liam would bring the necessary paper.

"If you do not," said the Authorities, "we will strike your name from the book."

When the men walked back to the village they were divided into two unhappy groups. Those whose names were written in the book. Those whose names were not.

My father Conall Mac Cormaic walked alone. Bitter.

Liam tried to walk beside him. My father's strides were angry and fast.

"It's six whole pence a day you'll have," Conall mocked him.

"I want to marry your daughter Roisin." That was how Liam O'Coffey asked for Roisin Mac Cormaic.

Like a prince, or a damned fool. Straight out in front of everyone.

Just as straight, we heard, our father stopped in the middle of the road, the flames from his chest scorching Liam's clothes.

"And you now a landless fool. Whistle your false music elsewhere!"

Whistle your false music elsewhere. I like that.

I am only a tiny bit sorry for Roisin Dubh when I see the sudden misery that curves her back and sucks the light from the air around her.

6

The next morning Liam O'Coffey looked one last time at the potato field his father Padraig and his grandfathers tended for centuries.

He filled his eyes with it, and his chest with the memory of his other, greater inheritance.

Until two hundred years ago his family had owned all of the lands that were now the Landlord's, and old Padraig O'Coffey, in defiance of the English Conquest, had bequeathed those lands to Liam on his deathbed.

Now Liam stood with his back to the little cottage where his father died.

His brothers Aengus and Barra lunge at him furiously, swinging their fists, but he fends off both.

Strides away. Not even looking back at Roisin, where she and I stood watching from our cottage door.

She almost ran after Liam. Our father Conall Mac Cormaic be damned. False music be damned. My sister was trembling with love and sorrow, and I pinched her hand to keep her awake.

Let Liam O'Coffey break his back to build an English road for her sake.

"It is love," Granya says.

"It is a fool," our father says. Today the O'Coffeys might as well climb into their own coffins.

But Liam was not the only one to leave our village that day.

Other families left, too.

The women and children cried and the men blamed themselves as they carried away their meager possessions.

"Will they go on the road?" I ask Roisin.

"They'll build hidden scalpeens, and live there so the men can build the government road. Don't worry. Tonight they'll return and drag away their timbers and their thatch."

"Liam, too?"

"He'll build a scalpeen. He'll live there, and we'll take him what we can."

Maybe they would be arrested for building scalpeens, which were against the law. Maybe we would be arrested for bringing Liam food.

I'd heard of two little girls who were in prison for giving an evicted old man a piece of bread.

I don't say this to Roisin.

We had nothing left but cabbage. I don't say this either.

But Granya does.

These days it is Granya who will say anything. She is angry about potatoes, and no potatoes. Cabbage, and too little cabbage. Worms in the cabbage. Even wild weeds.

"What about your stolen dress? You could sell it."

I expect her to slap me but Granya goes back to bed without a word.

She falls into a sleep full of strange fruit and wide gray water where only gulls can follow.

Later that same morning the Constabulary arrived with the Farmer and a Wrecking Crew.

I recognized the Farmer from the back of his head, which I'd often seen in the front row during Mass at our little church, sitting with his family.

The Farmer signaled those of our dwellings which were to be tumbled. Roisin said this was to prevent the return of the departing families.

I didn't care if it was a sin, I wished the Farmer would drop dead. Maybe I would tell him so.

But he only grew a little as he surveyed the land he now owned. Bought, opportunely, Brigid told us, from the Landlord.

The Constabulary beat on the latched door of the O'Coffey cottage.

No answer.

At the Constable's nod, two of the Wrecking Crew broke down the door, forcing it with their shoulders.

They dragged Aengus out fighting, and threw him into the yard. Barra walked out, slow.

The Farmer was gentle.

"We're short of men. It'll be a pound for you, Barra O'Coffey, if you assist the Wreckers."

"Barra," Aengus threatens.

Barra hesitates.

Then we watch as he goes to help the Wreckers tear down his own cottage.

When the roof and the walls of the cottage have fallen, the Constabulary and the Wreckers depart.

Aengus tries to stop him, but Barra breaks free and runs in front of the Farmer's speckled horse.

"My pound, sir!"

The Farmer rides on as if he is deaf.

Aengus picks up a stone from the rubble and holds it hard as he watches the Farmer ride away.

When he goes to throw it I can think only of the horse, a magpie pony I've visited often, secretly, in the Farmer's barn.

I'd seen the farmer spit on it mornings and at night to protect it from the fairies who hated anything that was soiled.

They say a speckled horse is a bad omen, and maybe it is true.

I am running towards the horse as the stone hits me in the forehead.

The world is red pain.

Then it is gone, and there is only a lovely field of white.

I laughed when I found the magic black box again so quickly.

It was balanced next to the two heavy carpetbags in the back of a horsedrawn cart on a street in Dublin.

The English Photographer was standing beside the cart.

Passersby stared, as curious as I am, at the strange new invention.

The Photographer was pretending to listen to a military officer, who was explaining patiently:

"Not only are the farmers and the provision dealers arming themselves, sir, but the devils who are working for five shillings a week are depriving themselves of food. Pooling their money and buying arms. If you must travel without military escort, do not travel unarmed."

The English Photographer was stubborn.

We smelled a bakery up the street. He emptied one of his carpetbags of clothing and toiletries, and took it in hand.

"Wait here with the camera," he told the officer. "I won't be long."

I wanted to stay with the magic box, too, but even more, I wanted to go with the Photographer to the bakery.

I hurried to keep up with him.

The surprised officer stared after us. A bell on the door jingled as I followed the Photographer into the bakery.

When we exited, the carpetbag was overflowing with bread. I carried a loaf of my own, soft, warm and already half-eaten.

I was so happy I almost forgot the magical machine. I was glad it hadn't been stolen.

"I am now properly armed," the English Photographer told the officer.

"Very good, sir." The officer was skeptical.

I bit more of my bread.

The officer watched the backs of our heads as we drove away through the crowded Dublin street.

We went to a soup kitchen. It was a huge cauldron in a dismal public building. A ragged crowd gathered with their empty tin cans in hand.

I only watched, because I had no tin can.

But I'd eaten my bread, and anyway the soup stank like sweat and the bones of drowned horses.

I looked at the English Photographer to see if he noticed this, but he was busy, his hands working over the magic box.

Then he disappeared under its black cape, as if he was hiding from us all.

The kitchen workers who were ladling the soup stared at the black box. I was proud to be standing next to it, an invention they had never seen before.

I tried to look at what the Photographer saw in his self-imposed darkness.

Some of those in the multitude cringed in shame.

They wanted us to take the black box somewhere else. To go away.

But most straightened and looked into the box with a calm and fierce dignity. As if they were conspiring with the Photographer and me.

When the Photographer emerged from beneath the box's black cape, his hair was wild. A thin little girl who looked like me moved out of our quiet black and white world.

Her dress was suddenly red, her bonnet blue. Her teeth stained green.

She approached the Photographer shyly, but her fascination gave her courage.

She spoke in Irish, which he could not understand:

"Do you wrestle with a spirit beneath the cloth?"

"Yes," I answer, importantly, for him. "He struggles with Death."

The utterly still black and white crowd disassembles in alarm.

The little girl's mother comes forward protectively, takes her arm. Leads her daughter away from the Englishman and our strange invention.

I didn't want to leave Dublin or the black box, but I woke up in my straw bed with a forehead that looked, Roisin said, as if a red cow bearing the weight of the world had stepped on it.

Old Brigid bathed the wound in herbs, and even Granya looked sorry for my head ache, and let my hair stay in fairy knots.

Only Little Mary and the white cat understood about saving the speckled horse.

Conall Mac Cormaic, it was said, had thrown lightning bolts that almost killed Aengus, who was already half-dead with shame over what he'd done.

Aengus brought me a big, heart-shaped potato that Roisin baked for me. It was stolen Granya said from God Knows Where, but I didn't care.

I was hungry in spite of the bread I ate when I went to the bakery with the Photographer.

Four days later, my head felt fine as hope, and I crept behind my father Conall on his way to the Farmer's barn.

I saw him stand, on his dark thin legs, only as humbly as a proud man not used to begging can.

The Farmer was disdainful of my tenant father.

I could smell it as clearly as I could smell the golden hay, and the wariness of the speckled horse: the Farmer coveted my father's half acre of land.

My father would not ask for much, he told the Farmer. He would work hard for him. Clear those fields that were now the Farmer's. Plant them when the time came, and whatever other work he'd have him do.

The Farmer looked around at his golden barn in a smug, self-satisfied way.

He wanted to know if Conall Mac Cormaic thought his barn looked like a Charity Workhouse. If my father wanted to work, he'd have to give up his half-acre. It was useless to my father now.

"Let others," the Farmer said, "put the land to better use. Your time is over. For the sake of the country."

"What country is that?" my father demands, in Irish.

"Ireland, Conall Mac Cormaic, Ireland!" The Farmer smiles in the language of Englishmen.

It is a language my father decides will never again live in his own mouth.

"No, not Ireland," my father growls, low. "You mean the country of greed, and setting yourself above your neighbors."

"Get out," the Farmer says. "Or I'll have you hung for a horse thief."

My father looks into the big eyes of the magpie pony and knows that we will starve. He does not blame the horse. He does not blame the land. He does not blame God.

It is the Farmer he curses.

"You show us our graves. But you won't be rid of us. We will rise up in the grass. We will rise up in the grass to curse you and your children's children."

7

Roisin **Dubh took off her leather shoes** and brushed them while she sang:

I have been given jewels of wondrous beauty. A pair of shoes fair, smooth and handsome, of leather made in white Barbary, and brought by King Philip's ships over the sea.

After she brushed her shoes, she polished them with a little rag. Only the white cat and I watched.

Granya had taken Little Mary to beg at the house of a farmer in a neighboring village, and Michael, I knew, was sleeping under a large oak up on the wooded hill.

He was ashamed to come home on most days.

The Roadworks Authorities would not hire him because he was the son of Conall Mac Cormaic who refused to give up his half acre. He found no work in any neighboring village except to join with the Housewreckers who were working for the Farmer as he bought up the land of the tenants who owed back rent.

If Michael raised the bone of one finger, our father Conall warned, to pitch in with the housewrecking, he would break every other bone in Michael's body, and that one raised finger he would saw off and feed to the blackbirds.

So Michael climbed the hill to sleep under the oak.

Purposefully, Roisin picks up her shoes and goes out, barefoot. She does not warn me to stay behind, so the white cat and I follow.

The little white cat, white, white, white, I sing. The little white cat, St. Brigid's cat. The little white cat, snowy white, who was drowned in a trench.

He does not like the song, so I carry him against my chest down the long road to the next village, where my sister hoped to sell her shoes.

"Rat," I whisper into his soft ears, to make him purr.

I hated rats.

The Norman ships brought rats to our country. They sucked the milk from the breasts of women who were nursing. A fat one had leapt for my mother's breast but she was strong and waiting, and killed it with a stone.

Only the verses of a true poet could drive rats away from a house or a village, my father Conall had told me.

Then they traveled in a herd, obedient to the verses, carrying away their ailing old king on a branch held between their razor teeth.

That made me laugh, and the white cat purr.

The next village, Roisin's shoes were admired, but no one had money or potatoes.

So we walked on.

My sister sang to shorten the road. A pair of shoes, valiant, splendid in public places. A pair of shoes, made of the hide torn from the white cow, the cow that was guarded in a desert palace, and watched over by a giant, with the utmost care.

The next village, we were lucky. Roisin hesitated only a little before she traded the shoes for a five pound sack of Indian meal.

"Thieves," I say under my breath, then aloud, so we had to leave quickly.

We returned at dusk. Granya was there, with a single egg that was given to Little Mary. Michael had come down from the hill, quiet, oak leaves in his hair.

Roisin poured some of the yellow meal into a boiling pot of water. We watched as she stirred it.

"What is it?" Granya asks.

"Indian corn meal. They eat it in America."

"I have heard it is poisonous!"

Michael mocks Granya. "Or we'll become Indians."

Roisin stirs the pot so it won't lump.

"I hope we don't become Indians," I say. "Others will try to kill us if we do. Or we will try to kill them back."

Our father comes home. He has no good news, so even Granya keeps quiet. He doesn't look at anything except the fire.

We know he is fuming, like all of the men, over the vapors of the blind volcanoes hidden deep inside the earth that rose up and destroyed the potato crops across Ireland.

Roisin pours the stirabout into a large bowl, and we gather around with our spoons.

Except our half-starved father. He walks out again, grim.

Maybe Roisin did not know how to cook the Indian meal. Or maybe it was because we weren't Indians, and had never been to America.

But not long after we ate the stirabout our stomachs twisted in pain. Michael swore he'd steal horses out from under the backsides of the Fianna themselves before he'd ever eat another mouthful of the strange porridge.

Everyone went to bed when the sun fell.

I went out to spy on Father Brennan.

I had not visited his sparse room in weeks. Maybe there would be a crisp potato peel on his supper plate.

There was not.

The priest, angrier than I had ever seen him, was composing a letter by candlelight.

He had more silver in his hair than since last Sunday's mass. His quill scratched the paper as it cursed Your Honors.

"It is clear," he grit out, "that the half-built roads shall not be finished as the men are barely kept alive by the rations they can afford."

He went on.

"These half-built roads shall scar the face of Ireland as an enduring reproach" --

His face turned red.

"-- to your idiotic policy."

He paused. I held my breath in case he should look my way. I was already nine years old, plugged my ears in church and had never been to confession.

"If the men are not freed," the priest warned, "to sow and plant the land for the next year's crop, all hope for their survival will be lost."

Suddenly I am afraid of what the priest will say next.

"They will sink," he declares, "into the land itself."

My scalp prickles and rises like a field. I remember my father's curse on the Farmer, that someday we would rise up from the grass.

Then Father Brennan looks straight at me.

But the man of God does not see me. I am only one little girl standing beside him.

Why should he see me, when he is seeing every village like ours in Ireland sinking into the land itself?

The men labored to build the strange and useless road that began and ended nowhere.

It went straight up the side of a barren brown hill.

They could not refuse to build it, or they would not be paid. So they laughed, some of them until they fell down dead, building that road.

They swung pick axes. They hauled stones.

More than the Roadworks Authorities, or the Overseer, more than the Queen of England, they hated the Ganger.

He walked among them cracking his whip near their backs without any expression. He was cruel without any expression and they hated him for that.

Later, he would be found dead, his head crushed by a pick axe, and by God, they said, he wore an expression then.

But not yet.

Liam, Aengus and Barra labored among the destitute men.

Roisin and Granya and I sometimes visited. We took the brothers boiled cabbage they had to get by diving into the bushes where we waited.

The Overseer, a man on the back of a white horse I'd never seen before, sometimes rode among the men.

A white horse does not live long. Aengus and Barra and some of the others would look at the Overseer and exchange sly glances.

Only the horse and I noticed.

Late afternoons the three O'Coffey brothers would stand in line with the multitude of other laborers. They were paid, one by one, with six pence and a small bag of Indian meal.

Early evenings I'd open the cottage door and find Indian meal and coins on the doorstep. Roisin and Granya would go to buy turnips or cabbage or leeks that our father Conall, thin as a shadow, would refuse to eat.

Nights, my dreams raged. I saw the Mollies, a mob of furious men, their faces blackened, dressed in women's clothing.

Aengus, a long whip in his hand, leads the Overseer's frightened white horse from the barn.

I want to run towards the horse and comfort it, but I can't move my legs or cry out.

Then the black-faced men set fire to the thatched roof of the Overseer's cottage. The Overseer, his wife and children come running out the door and stare at their blazing roof.

The Mollies drag away the Overseer. They tie him by the feet to a rope they fasten to the horse, then they crack the whip so that the white horse races away, dragging the man behind him.

"Follow your own Road to Nowhere, Your Lordship!" The Mollies call out.

Then we all run away.

The Roadworks Authorities announced that the work for the road was closed until the lawless men who set Mr. Smith's house ablaze with his wife and children in it, and who brutalized him before their very eyes, were found out.

Until the names of the criminals were known, the whole district would be punished. The O'Coffey brothers and the other laborers looked steadily at the Authorities, careful not to look at each other. But Father Brennan glared at everyone, furious.

On the road back to the village the men whose names had all been written in the Authorities' book now walked apart from each other.

Father Brennan, in the lead, was also grim.

The men would say nothing later, but we knew what happened on the road home.

Liam lunged for Aengus and brought him to the ground.

They wrestled.

The men of the village halted to wait the fight out. Expressionless as the Ganger, now. Even Father Brennan made no move to part the fighting brothers.

Liam and Aengus beat each other until their fury was weaker.

Then they lay in the road side by side. The other men, looking more satisfied, went their way.

We knew all of this because of how much lighter the men's hearts seemed when they arrived home. "The fools have forgotten," Roisin said, "they have no work now."

There would be no more coins on our doorstep.

All five of Conall Mac Cormaic's children crept towards the Farmer's field on a cold autumn night.

We knew our father would die of shame if he could see us.

Or break our bones and feed the worst ones to the blackbirds.

But it was dark and only the moon watched from on high.

Roisin carried a woven sack.

The windows of the Farmer's cottage were still lit from within, but no dog barked.

My sisters and my brother and I dug with our sticks into the soft earth, foraging forgotten turnips here and there.

"This is a sin," Granya whispers.

It is like saying, the night is cold, or, the stars are shining.

This is a sin.

An owl calls. I feel the wind of his brown wings fan my face.

"I am the oldest," Roisin Dubh whispers. "Let the sin be mine."

8

Father Brennan shouts at mass.

"The men of violence say we are starving wolves in our cabins, and it is time for us to unleash our fury."

Father Brennan shouts that we are not wolves, but Catholic men and women. Though the English Lords send away our country's grain in ships, and though they rejoice as our numbers disappear from the earth, we shall endure.

Tens of thousands of names of those dead of hunger are read in parishes across Ireland as he speaks, but those names will not be read in hell.

He reads the names of our own dead.

"Rejoice," the priest tells us. "For it is better to suffer one hundred years on this earth than to suffer one single moment of eternal damnation."

Aengus stands, his beard on fire. He spits on the church floor.

Liam's face whitens, but he makes no move to stop his brother.

Aengus walks out, his head high.

Granya is trembling.

Barra rises, follows his brother.

None of the O'Coffey brothers appeared at mass after that. Aengus and Barra walked somewhere east and were gone for days.

Liam, we knew, wandered over the Landlord's vast lands, checking his own secret snares, hopeful of a rabbit or a hare.

Liam must have been astonished that morning when he approached his snare, and saw, among all creatures, a stag standing noble as a king, one leg, somehow, miraculously, caught.

Some warned it was the ancient poet come back to curse the O'Coffeys, and they would not touch the meat.

Most said the stag was St. Padraig himself. St. Padraig had turned to an animal to sacrifice himself for us. The stag, Old Brigid told us, was Christ, who had come back to feed us once again.

Only Liam knew how it felt to grab Christ by the sharp antlers, twist his powerful head and cut his throat. I found the blood spot later, even after he had scrubbed it with snow and covered it with oak leaves.

When Liam walked back into the village with the bag of deer meat, no one saw him. He walked from cottage to cottage laying chunks of venison on our frozen doorsteps.

I followed his hoof prints as they pointed away from the village. They went a long way, back to his scalpeen.

Smoke and the smell of roasting meat rose from the hole in the thatch of his underground shelter near my feet. "Mary's wing over your head, Liam," I whisper, and race home.

Granya opened the door and found the meat on the doorstep. Picked it up quickly and brought it into the cottage.

I was disappointed. I'd wanted Roisin to find it.

"It was your man. God forgive him. He's stolen from the Landlord."

Roisin looked at our hungry faces. "Save God's forgiveness for those who need it more than my Liam."

Everyday we ate as much of the meat as we could stew in our kettle. Roisin was afraid to hide it in the snowbank next to our cottage, in case the Authorities came.

Our neighbors had the same fear, and did likewise. No one would have informed on Liam. Even our father Conall ate the stew without saying a bad word against the fool who'd given up his land to work on a Road to Nowhere.

But our father grew sick anyway.

He stayed in his straw bed.

He head ached and his back ached. His bones were stiff and he had a fever. His eyes, I thought, looked like two smoored coals.

When he was awake he no longer wanted to eat. I brought him water. He drank it. He looked through the open shutters and prayed, like Old Brigid, to the moon to grant us health and save us from wolves.

My father Conall had told us the last wolf in Ireland was killed sixty years ago. It had cursed us all before it died.

Somehow I knew my father mourned the wolf.

I laid my head against his chest and listened to his heart.

It told me it wanted to go on the road.

Not without me, Conall Mac Cormaic.

"What do you hear, Una?" My father climbs out of his fever.

I don't care if my tongue turns black and falls off.

I lie: "I only hear the snow fall."

When we were once again sure that our father Conall slept, Roisin Dubh put on her shawl and set her basket on her arm, not saying where she was going.

I waited, then slipped quietly out the door after her. High on the wooded hill I hid behind a tree and watched my dark sister wait for Liam.

They walked towards each other, frightened.

They hold each other warm, and as I watch, uneasy, I understand, for the first time, that this is love.

I don't like it.

She is and she isn't Roisin Dubh. He is and he isn't Liam. They are more than that.

They are like all the famous lovers I have heard of in stories.

Cuchulain and Emer.

Dairmaid and Grainne.

Oenghus and Caer.

They're living a story and it is not the one I wanted to tell, where it is only Roisin Dubh, my sister, and I together, forever.

It is a story that is, and isn't, their own.

They will leave our world and go somewhere together. I don't know where.

Now I'm more alone than I have ever been.

How can I blame them for going?

But I do.

Liam reaches into his cloak and pulls out a lovely pair of deer hide shoes he's crafted for my sister's feet.

She starts to cry.

He kneels and holds each frozen red foot in his hands, rubs it and slips it into its warm shoe.

"Sister, you have been given shoes of wondrous beauty," I whisper, angry. "A pair of shoes, fair, smooth and handsome, of leather made in white Barbary, and brought by King Philip's ships over the sea."

"I brought you turnips," Roisin tells Liam.

Her voice breaks and she starts to laugh, weakly, and I almost laugh, too. Liam wipes away her tear and I can feel its wetness on my finger.

They lay like two orphaned children on patches of dried leaves. I lean more closely to catch the words they whisper to each other. It is the same words I have heard them whisper before.

It is their old ritual.

Had I a team of horses then against the hills I'd plow. And preach a gospel during mass to my Little Black Rose. I would kiss the young maid when she'd first love to me vow, and savor splendor in the grass with my Little Black Rose. The Erne will be a torrent, hills will be laid low. Waves of blood will be the sea as blood the sky will flow. Every mountain glen in Ireland and bogs shall tremble so.

All this before I'd perish, your Little Black Rose.

I hoped their breaths mingled and froze solid in the cold. I left my sister and her lover laying warm on the frozen ground, turnips rolling between them.

I walked slowly back home.

Not in the hollows Roisin's feet made in the snow. I made small tracks of my own.

Granya was envious because of a wake for the neighbors' son Padraig tonight. He was sailing for America in two days.

"How can they afford whiskey and tobacco for a wake?"

"They are spending their coffin money." Granya was not afraid of Gray Man, the fog who liked to sink ships with red-haired women in them.

Father warned of Gray Man from his bed. "They say blood is thicker than water," he added, "but the ships to America are coffins."

"Better," said Roisin Dubh, "to go to the Workhouse than to abandon Ireland."

Then Father was angry with my oldest sister, too. "This land has been held by my forefathers for three hundred years. They lived through famine, and never abandoned the land. Besides, no one who holds land can be admitted to the Workhouse!"

Granya looked towards our little window, shuttered against the snow that rose halfway up the wall of our cottage.

"There is hope from the ocean, but none from the grave."

I know she is thinking of the pubic hair love charm that will cross the Atlantic next to Aengus's heart.

"Better to die in Ireland than faraway among strangers," our father shouts. I am afraid he'll set the straw of his bed on fire.

Michael says nothing. Maybe he wants to go to America, too.

"St. Brendan sailed to America and came home again with many apples," I offer.

"And there on the sea the devil showed him hell!"

There was no answering Conall Mac Cormaic.

Maybe I would go live with Old Brigid. Or I would build my own scalpeen and live alone on the wooded hill near the spot where I hid the white chickens.

I lay down in our straw bed even before the sun started to fall that day, and slept with my eyes and mouth wide open, Roisin Dubh said, to make me laugh, as if I were no longer Una, but an ugly changeling.

I found the black box.

It was travelling through distant villages in the English Photographer's horsedrawn cart.

We rode throughout Ireland, and everywhere we witnessed the same story.

The mass eviction of tenants that December of 1846, when I turned ten years old.

I saw right away that the magic of the black box would help no one, but the Photographer did not.

He looked through its eyepiece from first light until dark. We watched the agents on horseback as they rode into villages with their crews of Housewreckers, Sheriffs and Constabularies.

We listened as officers read aloud the names of those to be evicted.

Stubborn tenants who would not abandon their cottages were dragged out, and what little they possessed after selling all they had for food was thrown into the yard.

Sometimes the boards of a bed, or a stool. Sometimes an old kettle, or an empty, boat-shaped baby's cradle.

The English Photographer held steady in the chaos, even if his hands sometimes trembled when he lifted the box's cape and disappeared beneath it.

We watched young women and mothers, thin as my sisters, lament, pray and grovel.

Fall near the hooves of the nervous horses.

We saw the younger men threaten. Saw the old men and women, fearless, rage curses against the men on horses who were throwing them out to die.

The other children witnessed all of this, too. They ran to where their fathers and the other men were standing around outside, hard and dejected, looking inwards towards unbridgeable distances.

I huddled closer to the Photographer and the magic box.

We watched the Housewreckers, who everyone knows are grudges evicted from their own villages.

They tore down cottage after cottage across Ireland. They jumped onto roofs with saws. They tied ropes and the roofs of the cottages came crashing down.

The horses carried away the Authorities, and the tenants, broken, sat beside their ruined homes.

It was hard for the English Photographer when the tenants looked back at him, not liking or disliking him. Not seeing him at all.

After a while they moved away, dragging what they could of their sawed roof beams and thatch, to build their scalpeens.

Some stayed and built shelters they could only lie down in, beneath their fallen homes.

Some kissed the broken walls of their cottages before they took to the road.

Have you ever kissed a stone?

I wanted to die and take to the Hunger Road, too, wandering Ireland.

I climbed up next to the Photographer in his horsedrawn cart. I tried to close this invisible eye in my forehead.

It stayed open in spite of the red scar from Aengus's stone. It stayed open even when the light was gone and the Photographer was no longer looking through the black box.

It watched as a large family took to the snowy road, mourning.

The Photographer descended from the cart, taking his large carpet bag, and, I was relieved to see, the magic box.

I descend, too.

The horse is as astonished as I am when the Englishman hands the cart over to the man of the family on the road.

I say good-bye to the horse.

Now we will go on foot over the snowy roads.

The English Photographer talks to the woman named Mary who is waiting in England.

Mary, he is lost.

He can no longer bear the blue staring eyes of children like skeletons.

He feels Henry's box can help no one. He is ashamed.

He is utterly ashamed to be the subject of a Queen who, it was said all over this country, tell him it is not true, has offered a mere five pounds to this famine.

If his journey through Ireland will make a difference, he is afraid that difference will come far too late.

Mary, these are his Christmas tidings.

He has seen the spirit of Christ broken on Christmas Eve. The most sacred night of the year.

9

Our father, sick in his bed, turned a strange, dusky color. "Road fever," Old Brigid said.

She brought dried shamrocks, sorrel and vervain, but they did not cure Conall Mac Cormaic.

On the fifth day he began to shake with cold, and a rash appeared on his shoulders and abdomen. His face swelled, and when he spoke to us he was like a drunk man.

He shook and often shouted of things we didn't understand.

We knew he had gone with the fairies.

Conall Mac Cormaic tattooed himself and rode stolen horses. Killed and cursed his way from far off plains to Ireland.

He pissed himself and dropped priceless illuminated manuscripts as he ran from yellow bearded Viking bastards.

He stole a sainted boy named Maewyn.

Sold him to a farmer in Antrim, not knowing the slave was St. Patrick.

When handbells rang, my father hid in towers, trembling like a lamb even high above the invaders.

He kissed the rouged nipples of the whore who killed our only great king, Brian Boru.

He disguised himself as a Norman and married an Irish noblewoman, who persuaded him to sire many children and build as many churches.

Conall Mac Cormaic foolishly agreed to become six thousand Irish soldiers fighting an English war against Scotland, and his reward was a moaning white cow with dry udders.

So he turned himself to a flea that leapt from a rat in an Irish port and carried the Black Plague to the English.

Then he turned himself to a wolf carrying an axe and howled at the feet of Queen Elizabeth and did even not leap for her powdered throat.

My father loved innumerable Irish women who kissed men who were not their husbands, who drank more whisky than he could, and who divorced their husbands if the black mood struck them.

Then Conall Mac Cormaic drunkenly advised one hundred other lords to sail away from Ireland and leave their estates to the English.

He beat, stripped and sent Protestants into the wilderness to die.

Even if they spoke his native tongue.

He cut off the breasts of Protestant women and cut the throats of Protestant children and threw them in the Bann River.

He somehow escaped, charred, from the burning church at Drogheda, and did not drag a single soul along with him.

He let himself be driven to the barren lands of Connacht. Abandoned his promising crop of wheat to Cromwell's soldiers.

It was he, Conall Mac Cormaic, who hid cowering in the hedgerows.

Who stepped out, blackened his face and wore white smocks over his clothes. Who grew a heart of oak and wore an oak sprig in his hat.

Raked torturous carding combs over the faces of Landlords, and later went to mass.

It was he who joined the United Irishmen and then grew frightened and hid underground. My father who handed Wolfe Tone the pen knife so he could cheat the English Hangman.

Conall Mac Cormaic had not attended the meeting at Clantarf.

It was he who advised O'Connell to take the pilgrimage to Rome, to look for refuge in a foreign land, not knowing that only the great heart, in a box, without its exhausted leader, would reach Rome.

For all of these things Conall Mac Cormaic begged forgiveness.

He had murdered our mother, too, by giving her Little Mary, and for this, above all, he begged forgiveness.

All he wanted was her voice that came through the honey.

We sat around him, in terror at his battles.

He struggled to come back to us. He steadied himself as if he were on a boat. He spoke to us as if he were calling across water.

He told Roisin not to give up the land.

"Take Una and Little Mary to the Workhouse at Athlone."

At Athlone they would not know we were tenants, and there we would eat.

"No," I shout.

He told Roisin to bring us home next harvest, when there would be plenty. No one except me wanted to contradict Conall Mac Cormaic on his deathbed.

We sat around him, our breaths visible in the cold air. Roisin had opened the door for the departure of his spirit, and Michael had opened a hole in the roof thatch.

Father Brennan stepped softly in. He blessed everyone except the cat, who did not care, and he glared at Granya, who he suspected of helping the Mollies.

The priest attended our father gently. "I will hear your confession, Conall Mac Cormaic."

"He is going to heaven," I say, "He has already confessed. He murdered Daniel O'Connell and our mother."

They ignore me.

"Here before my children?" my father almost laughs, but his lips are too swollen.

I see a little of the old lightning in his hands. I bring him his pipe. He sticks it, unlit, between his teeth.

"I'll take my sins to the grave," he tells the pipe, "and enjoy them twice first."

The priest does not like that. He motions us out of the cottage. We do not want to go. I want to light my father's pipe first. There are no sparks left in his thumbs.

But the man of God is fierce.

We want our father to take us with him in his death boat. We want to cross the water with him.

But we go. When Father Brennan closes our cottage door and turns back to Conall Mac Cormaic he finds him triumphant. Because our father's undying spirit has escaped through the hole in the roof.

They lowered his body into its grave through a trap door coffin.

Our father had spent his coffin money to buy us potatoes as dear as gold, and now he was in a box that only looked like a coffin of his own.

The bottom swung open like a door and dropped Conall Mac Cormaic into a dark hole.

I plugged my ears so I would not hear his body thud against the earth. Only the gravedigger, Father Brennan, Old Brigid, Roisin, Granya, Michael, Little Mary and I were present.

The Authorities were searching for the O'Coffey brothers, so Liam kept hidden in his scalpeen. Aengus and Barra had walked east again, over the wooded hill. Our neighbors kept away, too, because they feared the road fever.

We departed quietly from our father's hole in the earth. Old Brigid and my sisters too weak to keen.

I mourned because the magic box had not made its way to our village.

I would never see my father's face in a glass world.

There would be no wake. No whisky, no tobacco. No stories about the many lives and deaths of Conall Mac Cormaic. No music. No tears. No stifled laughter.

Only our silence.

It was the same silence that covered the Irish countryside, as killing as the Great Hunger.

On the way home I kept looking back, hoping to see my father, mute and distant, smoking the pipe he'd light with sparks from his thumbs.

I did not.

I saw something gray, standing at an angle to us, turn and walk slowly west, as if it did not want to go.

"Father," I called. "Come get your pipe." Roisin Dubh held my hand tightly.

When I'd told her I wanted to die, too, she made me drink a tea of evil herbs, and threatened to press my hand to a hot kettle.

I was not sure if I was cured.

Granya looked back at the gray ghost and started to cry. "He never loved me."

"He loved you best," Roisin Dubh said. Was it a lie?

Father Brennan warned us, the next mass, of another blight over our land.

It was the Protestants.

And when the Protestant comes, ever so kindly, with his bread and his soup in exchange for our Catholic soul, would we abandon it, the only eternal being God has given us, simply to satisfy our temporary, worldly hunger?

"For," he warned, "those who partake of this poisonous soup not only curse themselves, but their villages, for seven generations."

We looked at each other, the fading number of our congregation.

We were worse than ragged in the few clothes we had not sold for cabbage or turnips or Indian meal.

But we were all determined we would not be the one to curse our village.

Everyone that is, except Roisin Dubh.

The next day she took Little Mary and I to the neighboring village. Michael roused from his bed under the oak leaves on the wooded hill and came with us.

On the path to the village Roisin walked fast and said nothing. "Shorten the road," I begged.

But she would tell no story.

We came to a building where several Quakers in their odd dress were administering soup to a ravenous crowd.

I could feel my dark sister, who was holding my hand, begin to tremble.

I saw the hair stand up on her arm.

A Quaker woman looked at us kindly through the open doorway.

Roisin Dubh's face burned sudden red, and she turned away. Dragging us with her.

Little Mary, who had smelled the soup, began to cry.

Michael cursed. The bastard man of God was lying. The priest would kill us to save our souls.

Was Father Brennan's left ear burning?

"Seven generations," Roisin Dubh warned. My brother followed us over the cold path home.

That night in our cottage, my older sisters lay awake. I listened with my eyes closed, feigning the rise and fall of sleep.

Granya whispered that Roisin Dubh had almost cursed us.

Roisin sounded bitter. She was not at all sorry. Maybe she would even go back, and curse us for sure.

Because there was no curse in saving children.

"Our neighbors would revile us."

"Our neighbors are dying."

"If we blacken our names," Granya warned, "we might as well die, too. We couldn't go to mass. Even my own Aengus might not marry me."

"His love is a small one," Roisin whispered, "if he carries your pubic hair near his heart, but would rather see you dead than taking the soup."

That made Granya furious. She thought of Aengus spitting on the church floor, and of the shorn love locks, and wept.

"What would we say to Father Brennan? Yes, Father, we're Protestant now, but only until the potatoes grow."

Roisin saw no use in the quarrel. "We must put our hope in the next harvest."

Granya said it was folly to trust in the land any longer. She would go to America with Aengus.

Roisin was the oldest, and she forbade Granya to go. "One sister is worth more than seven husbands."

Granya said that was true.

I did, too.

"Go to sleep, Una," they scolded. "Stop your spying."

I closed my eyes. They did not love me.

I saw seven Liams, all stepping forward together to accept my dark sister's hand if she would offer it. Go away, Liam, I tell the suitors, and then I am truly sorry.

Because the Liams turn to seven stags noble on the wooded hill, and then to seven blood soaked places in the snow.

I made my way back to the O'Coffey scalpeen when the sun was just over Old Brigid's chimney.

I was careful to walk backwards half the way, and to circle around, too, in order to confuse the Authorities in case they were searching.

I spied down through the brush and saw Liam, gaunt, before a tiny peat fire. Aengus and Barra, returned from their long walk east, looked strong.

Barra handed Liam a small bag with a few potatoes in it. Liam pocketed two of the potatoes to give to Roisin, and ate the third raw.

Aengus opened another bag and took out a large and shining object. He had found a leprechaun's secret store. It was a silver candelabra.

He sets it on a large stone and lights its candles with sparks from his thumbs.

I want to cry, remembering my father Conall.

Aengus says the candelabra will pay their way to America.

"It is cheaper to go to Canada," Barra offered, as if now he had a beard and knew too much about strange lands.

Aengus scorned that country. Canada was only another Ireland, with her Queen and her Lords.

Liam shook his head like a stag at his brothers. "There is no other Ireland on this great earth."

So thought my father Conall.

Without warning, Barra, pretending to be a man now, blew out one of the candle flames.

As if it were his own life.

He hands the candelabra to Aengus. "Take it as a wedding gift."

Liam and Barra would stay in Ireland.

Aengus would cross the ocean with his Granya. She wouldn't need to sell the stolen green dress. Granya would wear it and drink whisky at her wedding.

Had the O'Coffey brothers forgotten green was unlucky for a bride?

10

We gathered nettles in the solitary graveyard near the stones that marked where a chapel had once been.

"The best nettles grew over the dead," Old Brigid told us.

She showed Roisin Dubh, Granya and I how to grasp nettles so they would not sting our hands. We are fearful at first, and sting our hands anyway.

Old Brigid scolds us for our gentleness. "Hold the tall green plants hard. Pull them straight out of the earth."

I pretend I am an English giant, walking over Ireland, tearing up trees with my bare hands.

"When we had plenty," grumbled Old Brigid, "we gave it no thought. We had so many we left them in the ground, or threw them into ditches to rot."

We know she is talking about potatoes. I wish she would not.

I know the nettles will make all of our stomachs twist and will make us run from the cottage with diarrhea.

But Old Brigid has a soup bone and needs something to add to the pot.

She drank nettle tea often when she was a girl, and it put fine roses in her cheeks. "Don't stare," Roisin nudges me.

But when I look hard at Brigid's ancient face, the roses are still there.

We gather nettles in silence, and I begin to hear it:

A heavenly music.

It rises like a birdsong, or the voice of a woman singing in the language of birds.

I feel something inside my head lift and go up into the air, and I see out over Ireland from my high branch.

I drop my basket, looking around, and Old Brigid sees me. Says, approvingly: "You hear the beautiful singing?"

I nod.

"That's St. Brigid. When I was a girl I'd come here to hear her sing, too."

Old Brigid, my sisters and I pause in a deep, listening silence.

Granya elbows Roisin as if to say the old woman has gone with the fairies.

Roisin shushes her. Rises from her knees, because she can almost hear St. Brigid singing, too.

I felt the way I knew I would if only I could see my mother's face.

Suddenly, a wild goose flew out of the tall grasses. I ran towards the place where it had rested.

It was a miracle.

A nest of six, perfect eggs.

Fourteen days later, I was as hungry as if I'd never eaten my egg.

Granya threatened to sell the green dress. Roisin was afraid it would bring the Authorities to our cottage.

My sisters sold their petticoats instead.

They complained their rounded breasts and hips had disappeared. Now their chests were thin as mine. Their eyes huge.

I heard them whisper to each other they had stopped their bleeding, too. Now there were no rags to wash in the river. They were no longer women. They didn't know what they were. They went to Old Brigid.

"Of course you are women," she scolded. "Your cycles will return."

They sold our wooden bowl. Then our wooden spoons.

They didn't speak of Liam or Aengus or Barra. No one knew where they were. The O'Coffey scalpeen was empty.

Then one evening Liam appeared with a half-roasted joint of meat and a badly burned hand.

Roisin tore her one remaining petticoat to bandage the wound. We knew that Liam, welcomed into a Stranger's kitchen as he looked for work, lifted the meat from the spit over the fire when the housekeeper bustled into another room.

Grateful, we asked no questions.

Granya was hurt because Aengus stayed away. We wondered if he still carried the pubic hair love charm.

Through the glass pane window of their cottage, the Farmer and his wife and children were gathered around a table laden with bread, buttermilk and steaming potatoes.

Their heads bowed, they spoke a Catholic blessing before they began to eat their evening meal.

As the dishes were passed around, the Farmer eyed his oldest son, a listless boy my brother Michael's age, with hair combed free of oak leaves.

"Put more on your plate," the Farmer tells him.

"I am not hungry, Dad."

The Farmer grew angry.

Blessed as they were by God, and his son was not hungry. His son did not want to be among the lucky.

His son would rather be on his knees staining his mouth green with grass like the rest of the cursed.

The Farmer's Wife grew angry, too, but at her husband. Their son had felt poorly all day.

The Farmer looked more closely at his son, praying. "No, no sign of fever."

He quelled his alarm and went back to his plate.

Then the youngest child looked straight at the hole of my breath on the glass pane and cried out that the Hunger Fairy was at the window.

The Farmer's Wife stood. Quietly took a potato from her plate and hid it in the fold of her skirt. Left the table.

I waited in the darkness.

The Farmer called after his wife. "Give away what is ours and kill your own to save others."

Not long after that, Old Brigid opened a vein in the neck of her white cow, Niamh of the Golden Hair. Roisin caught the flowing red blood in a wooden basin. When the bowl was almost full, Brigid closed the vein with the magic of her fingers.

She patted old Niamh affectionately. I pressed my ear to the cow's great heart, worried she had died standing.

Her heart beat on.

Old Brigid and Roisin went into the old woman's cottage and cooked nettles and Niamh's blood together in a pot on the hearth. The smell nauseated Granya, who ran outside, past me, to vomit.

"What do I do, Brigid?"

I heard Niamh's heartbeat with one ear, and Roisin's question with the other.

"What do I do? If I don't take the girls to the Workhouse, they may die."

No. I will my own heart to stop a beat as I wait for Old Brigid's answer.

She is only the one who remembers the stories of our village, she reminds Roisin. She is not the one who tells which way the story should go.

"Tell it anyway," I whisper to Niamh.

If I open and close my eyes seven times, I tell myself, Brigid will keep Little Mary and I out of the Workhouse.

One, two, three, four, five, six, seven.

Old Brigid has seen this hunger back in her time. Little children suffered, then, too. Not everyone would survive. What part of Ireland's tree would bloom, what part would die?

Who would live to tell the story?

We did not know.

Last night Old Brigid dreamed of a priest who grew and grew into a giant, scouring all of Ireland for his supper.

The old woman and I had had the same dream.

Roisin's voice is hushed and somber. "To dream of a priest is bad. They say it is better to dream of the devil." It was worse than her own dream of wandering the roads of old Ireland.

Granya, pale, goes past me and back into the cottage. Ignores the pot of blood and nettles. "Your dream wasn't Father Brennan. He gives away his supper. Last night I dreamed the Pope sold the treasures of the Vatican to save us from this Hunger."

"You surely were dreaming." Old Brigid stirs the pot.

"The Pope could save us."

"The Pope has fled his own country."

"Father Brennan is thin as a dry grass stalk," Roisin mourns.

"We will all turn to dry grass stalks," Old Brigid warns. "But unlike the priests, we must never forsake the land."

That night I lay awake as long as Roisin did, then longer. She was troubled in the darkness. She turned to Granya.

No.

I felt the silver threads she'd woven between us with her stories break as if they were only the fragile webs of the white spider I was sure sometimes crept from my mouth while I slept.

No.

"I'll bring them home," I heard my beloved sister whisper. "I'll bring them home when the harvest comes in."

11

The road to the Workhouse was longer than any road I'd traveled.

I mourned because my white cat had gone hunting and I had not said good-bye.

We walked from the first light to dark. Slept beside the road, then woke and walked another day. Roisin often carried Little Mary on her back, and when her back got tired Little Mary walked between us.

We were only to look at the road ahead of us, not towards the grassy expanse to its sides where human souls had fallen, their mouths stained green.

No matter how hungry we were, we were not allowed to complain, and we were not allowed to touch the grass.

I no longer knew my sister Roisin Dubh. She had become a dark Evil Fairy. I did not want to listen to her.

My legs ached. My bare feet hurt from the stones in the road. My throat swelled and clogged with tears.

My Roisin had disappeared and left behind the ugliest woman I'd ever seen. This dark woman even carried a birch switch she threatened to cut our legs with if we stopped to rest before she said we could.

I tried to make her laugh to force the fairy away. I bared my backside and wiggled it, but she stayed grim. Snapped at it with her birch switch.

"Damn you." I told her. "You are the fairy changeling. I'll roast your hand in fire and bring back my Roisin Dubh."

She slapped my mouth.

After that, to spite her, I looked to the right of the road and to the left and even up at the sky.

Anywhere except the road itself.

But I regretted it.

Half-clothed skeletons, starved or dead of fever, lined the sides of the road, their mouths stained with grass. A black dog wandered, feeding on dead bodies.

The Evil Fairy picked up a stone and hurled it at the dog, who wouldn't scare.

I stopped to stare at a little girl who looked like me, except her nose and lips were blue and her eyes were deeper. Ravens pecked at her stomach.

The Evil Fairy pinched my arm, and we kept walking.

Miles ahead, we passed a Death Cart.

The driver was dragging bodies into the cart. He didn't say hello to us, and we pretended not to see him. Even after he was far behind us, I wouldn't look back. I didn't want to see the girl who looked like me waving from the Death Cart.

I looked at the sky. Maybe Gray Man would come and blind us in a fog. Make us lose our way.

No matter what, the Evil Fairy told Little Mary and I harshly, not a word from our mouths. Until she returned for us, we would only open our mouths to eat.

She grew angrier with us and walked faster until we were flying. We struggled to keep up.

Then she stops.

She holds our shoulders hard, spins us around to stare down the long road.

"Look back. Remember the way we are going because someday when the fields are blossoming you will walk back this way."

She promised she would be waiting. She would open the cottage door for us.

"It might be a long time from now," she warned. We would all be changed. But we were not to forget the way home.

"Because if you forget your true home," she told us, "you become no one."

We reached the Workhouse gates.

I tried to run away, but my oldest sister caught me.

Then I saw the English Photographer, grim, exiting the gates with the black box. He was exhausted. The black box had grown heavier.

Roisin Dubh looked past the Englishman, but I twisted towards him, not wanting to lose sight of the magic box.

"What is that strange black box?" I ask Roisin Dubh. I want her to see it, too. I want to tell her about its magic.

She presses her mouth shut.

I heard a wise old man sitting at the gate. He said to the air that the black box is a machine invented by the rich. It collects sunlight in order to make gold.

I try to tear away and go after the departing Photographer.

"Come back, sir," I call out. "Look at Roisin Dubh through your magic box."

But Roisin hurried Little Mary and I through the opened gate.

As she dragged us to the Workhouse doors, I heard a quarrelsome old woman contradict the old man.

"How much sunlight would he be finding in the Workhouse? Everyone knows the black machine's a cure for the dying. If you but sit near it and look into its eye, it cures your disease."

In the Workhouse Reception room my oldest sister's tongue turned black with lies. She told the official that her neighbor and her neighbor's husband had died, leaving Little Mary and I orphans. That we had no one to care for us.

Liar.

She had brought us here, not wanting us to starve.

The Official was suspicious, and wanted to know our names.

Then she wanted to know Roisin Dubh's name, and Roisin told her that Old Brigid was her mother and that her father had died long ago at sea.

The Official asked me if Roisin Dubh was indeed my neighbor.

No, she is an evil fairy.

I look at her and don't say a word.

"The children no longer speak. The Hunger has stolen their tongues."

I hold Little Mary's hand and pierce my oldest sister with blue needles from my eyes.

The Official looks resigned. She writes our names in a huge book.

My own Roisin Dubh had betrayed me.

My invisible eye watched her as she rushed through the Workhouse gates. She was sick over abandoning us.

I was glad.

She ran through the street and stumbled against the English Photographer's camera as she passed him.

"Watch your step, Englishman!" she admonished, her cheeks hot with fury. Then hurried on.

Roisin Dubh disappeared onto the lonely roads of Ireland. No one knew her face, or her name.

I had no reflection of my sister in a glass world.

When I lost sight of her I lost everything.

The barred window shattered into light I tried to gather in my hands.

Then I fell into the white field, leaving even Little Mary behind me.

I woke not too far from our village, in the Landlord's elegant dining room.

His wife and their children sat at a long table spread with silver and glass and strange foods.

Their candelabras, like the one from Aengus's bag, were lit, and portraits of their illustrious ancestors graced the walls, looking at us as if they hear rumors they do not like.

The Landlord's wife was furious, but his children exuded a natural joy. They were speaking, like the English Photographer, in a language I don't understand.

Then I swayed and the colors of the walls deepened, like their syllables, and I knew what they were saying.

The Landlord's youngest daughter, who looked like me except she wore a blue silk dress, asked, "Father, if we go to England, can we take our wild swans with us?"

The other children looked hopeful, too.

The Landlord pointed his chin at his furious wife and said, gently as the thud of their spoons on the cloth covered table:

"We are not returning to England."

His wife and his oldest daughter, whose green dress was not stolen, looked at him with venom.

He returned to his elegant meal.

Only then did we see the young stranger in ragged clothing who was standing in a corner of the room, surveying their feast.

His thin, ghostlike appearance was in contrast with the brilliant surroundings.

He was barefoot, and there were oak leaves in his hair.

It was my brother, Michael Mac Cormaic.

Dignified, he walked over to the table and bowed a little, as if to his equals. He took a plate and circled the table, loading his dish with pheasant and vegetables.

The Landlord's family and I watched in stunned silence.

I wanted to brush the oak leaves from his wild hair.

Michael seated himself at table and poured himself a glass of wine.

The Landlord's wife rose in outrage, but her husband gently motioned for her to stay calm. She sat down again.

I looked into the huge mirror on the wall and saw everyone, except my brother and I, reflected in it.

Where were we?

Michael spoke in Irish, which, I judged by their blank faces, they clearly do not understand.

"Pardon me if I speak to you in the language of my country. When I didn't get your invitation to dinner, I thought it would be rude not to invite myself. With the country suffering as it is and all, and you our guests here for seven hundred years."

Michael tasted his wine and it was strange in my mouth.

"Good," he nodded. "Almost as good as poteen."

He raised his glass in a toast, and only the youngest daughter corresponded.

"Here's to Jail," he toasted. "One pound of meal a day. It was that or the Workhouse. They give you potatoes and milk there.

But I was never one for the charity. Like you," he explained, "I'd rather steal."

He savored their strange food, and I was no longer hungry.

"Very, very good," he said between bites, "twice stolen food."

The Landlord's wife uttered a cry. Jumped up and ran for help. I ran, too, but no one ran after me.

The Landlord and his children sat quietly, watching Michael Mac Cormaic eat as he waited for his Jailers.

We were hypnotized by the spectacle of my starving brother.

12

When I found the black box again it was making its way over a long, winding country road in distant Ireland.

The English Photographer carried it on his back as he went on foot, along with his cumbersome bag. He didn't recognize me as the little girl led through the Workhouse gates as he rushed blindly out.

He saw the lonely road ahead, and he saw to the right of the road, and to the left, but he didn't see me at his side, struggling to match his long steps.

I looked at the big, fine, dusty boots that covered his tired feet. After a while I got bored of no one to talk to, so I riddled the Photographer.

"Two brothers we are, great burdens we bear in which we are bitterly pressed. The truth we do speak, we are full all the day, and empty when we go to rest."

He kept going.

"It's your boots, Englishman, it's your boots."

I walked close to the black box.

I had not seen it cure anyone's disease, or turn sunlight to gold, but I didn't care. I knew there was no invention like the magic box, and when the Photographer hid beneath its cape and looked through its eyepiece, I didn't have to look through my invisible eye anymore.

Someone else was seeing, too, and I was not alone.

I knew the Photographer was making a strange world of glass that reflected the world we were seeing. I had seen the glass world when he opened his carpet bag. The bread had disappeared from the carpet bag a long time ago, but I knew the glass world that had taken its place was important, too.

It is as if the English Photographer carried a bag full of lakes, or mirrors, where he had caught the escaping spirits of everything in my country that was dying.

The world he caught in the mirrors was in reverse. What was dying was living. What was dark appeared light. What was light turned dark.

If the Photographer looked at Roisin Dubh through the black box, in the glass world her hair would be long and pale as my own. Her eyes glowing like white suns. If he looked at me, my hair would be long and black as Roisin Dubh's.

But he had not been to our village.

Dead families lay stretched on the grass of the roadsides, their hands and mouths stained green. Sickened, we walked on. I saw the Photographer was tired of looking through his eyepiece.

We watched a spectacular butterfly where it lit on the cold blue forehead of a dead mother who lay with her children around her.

The butterfly had flown from her mouth, so I didn't try to catch it. They say butterflies are the soul of the dead, so we must not touch or harm them.

We walked on.

We saw a small cottage that somehow still stood among a ruin of tumbled cottages. We both wondered at the smoke rising from the chimney.

We went to the door, and knocked. I hoped they would mistake us for the Hunger Fairy, and give us something to eat.

No one answered.

We went in and found a small, cheery fire on the hearth.

For a moment we're relieved. Almost happy.

Then we turn and see a cheerful, emaciated woman who sits, as if in life, but dead, on a nearby stool, a teakettle in her hand.

A proud, once vigorous man stands in a corner as if alive, yet dead, his muddy spade in hand.

Six children sit at a table, joyous and also dead, around an empty bowl, their mouths stained green.

I close my eyes and sway. I want to faint but I can't. My invisible eye stays open.

Trembling with horror, the English Photographer goes beneath the black box's cape and looks through its eyepiece.

We look and look at the room and its still occupants.

I know we are seeing the same tableau: a way of life, an Ireland, forever gone.

Later, bootless under the cold stars, the English Photographer talks to Mary.

I try on his boots. My numb feet are lost in them.

He longs to go home but he does not know how. He does not know if he is fit, anymore, to go home to her or their child.

Maybe it is born and it is the daughter they longed for.

The Photographer feels beyond Mary's love here in Ireland.

He feels beyond all protection and prayer. His thoughts, he tells her, are black beyond all redemption.

I take off his heavy boots and set them near where he lays.

He had hoped the black box would change the world.

Now he knows it will not and he does not want to carry the weight of the heavy box any longer.

He looks at the magic box and is not strong enough to break it.

I shiver in the cold. I cup my hands over my mouth and blow to warm them.

"Don't break the magic box," I beg. "Even if it helps no one."

The Photographer does not listen. He is afraid that the magic box is going to break him, first.

I hear a tiny ringing in my ear. I know I must go home, but I wake up standing on the side of a snow covered hill.

Two armed men are chasing Aengus and young Barra and other Mollies towards me.

The men and I are running.

They are carrying stolen lambs too frightened to bleat. Barra runs past me, and then a shot rings out and a red stain spreads over his back. I watch as he falls on his face in the snow.

The black lamb he was carrying runs off to find its mother.

Aengus is still running with the white lamb. He turns to look for Barra.

The other Mollies disappear over the top of the hill.

An armed man shoots his rifle at Aengus, who is frozen in horror at the sight of Barra turning the snow red.

The armed man's shot kills the lamb in Aengus's arms. But Aengus doesn't drop the lamb. He rocks it like a baby.

The other armed man curses the one who shot Barra and the lamb.

"Running men are not wolves, damn you. I told you to shoot over the starving bastards' heads."

"And have them back again and us the worse off?" the cursed one spits.

Aengus is still holding the dead lamb tightly.

He stumbles downhill towards Barra and the armed men.

I search through the snow for the fallen pubic hair love charm until my fingers are stiff and red, and then until they no longer feel, and my tears turn to ice on my cheeks.

I could not find it.

Aengus O'Coffey gave himself up to the Hangman.

I wanted to go home but I woke up in the huge, dreary dining hall at the Workhouse.

The matrons, fearing my lice, had cut off my long yellow hair. Then they had shaved my head and stuck it in lime.

I hoped they would not throw the hair to the wind. If birds made their nests from your hair, Old Brigid warned, you would get headaches.

I had not cried. St. Brigid told me that in heaven no one had hair anyway.

My head felt weightless.

Little Mary and I sat, crowded onto benches with a multitude of other children. Obediently spooning our breakfast of oatmeal and milk into our mouths.

Talking, it was clear, was strictly forbidden.

I smiled at my sister. I didn't know if it was against the rules. Her little head was shaved, too, but her small face had grown round again, and there were dimples in her hands.

A stern matron patrolled the aisles between the tables.

I didn't dare whisper where I had been or how much I had missed my little sister.

That night, in the tiny bed Little Mary and I shared in a row of wooden bunks covered with clean straw, I raised a stolen candle above my head to see it more plainly.

I went down into the hold of a ship headed for Australia.

The Hangman's noose had slipped and lost Aengus, who was in chains.

There was no room to stretch out his long O'Coffey legs there in the filthy straw among a multitude of other convicts.

It was later said that Aengus broke out of prison and fought the English soldiers on Vinegar Hill. Ravens ate his eyes before he died.

Some said he escaped in the clothes of a high-ranking English officer and went to America where he was scalped by Indians, and survived.

Aengus, they say you became a cowboy and sang lullabies to wild horses in Texas. That you died of dysentery in a Union Camp in the north, carrying the green flag of Erin proudly through a hailstorm of bullets at Appomattox.

You joined the San Patricios in New Mexico Territory. Fought the Saxons and escaped into Old Mexico with a beautiful Spanish lady, where your red-haired descendants hide still.

Others swear on Christ's blood Aengus O'Coffey became a ditch digger who got drunk at night in Paddytown, or that he died working on the railway.

Others claimed he rioted in New York, destroyed its shops, and burned down an orphanage where he murdered fifteen black children.

Most spit at these lies.

Aengus O'Coffey struck a gold vein in California, and in the spring he will return in a fine suit to restore the glory of Ireland.

I myself never saw Aengus O'Coffey again.

I knew I had to go home, but when I made it back to the cottage they ignored me.

My white cat was there. I could tell by his swollen belly and smug look he had been out hunting Norman rats. He purred and wrapped himself around my feet.

The little white cat, white, white, white. The little white cat, St. Brigid's cat. The little white cat, snowy white, who was drowned in a trench.

Roisin sat on my stool before a peat fire, holding Granya close.

Granya also saw Aengus chained in the stinking hold of the ship, and she clutched the stolen dress as if it were her lover. My sister's unruly red hair had gone white, and her locks were greasy and tangled.

She wanted to die but she rocked herself instead.

Roisin stroked Granya's white tangles, and I kissed her cold, wet cheek but she didn't look at me. She was mute with sorrow for her lover.

The next day I followed Roisin and Granya when they carried the stolen dress to a distant town. We arrived in the afternoon.

Doors closed in our faces, as, one by one, the townswomen examined the wondrous dress, looked at my sisters' rags and bare feet.

"No."

Then at another door an old townswoman fingered the fine fabric. She looked sagely at Granya and asked its price.

Granya wanted no less than three pounds. The price of passage to America.

The old woman told my sisters to go see the Tinkers who were camped to the west of town. We would see their wagon. So we set off in the direction of the falling sun.

We found the brightly painted wagon where it set along the river.

I saw right away that the Tinker Woman had no children. Her breasts were small, and she had wrapped a large turnip in a blanket and was rocking it.

Her husband stirred a pot of stew, made from other turnips, over their cooking fire.

The Tinker Woman saw me right away but she said nothing about it. She lay the turnip aside and waited for my sisters to speak.

Roisin hung back, shy, but Granya stepped forward with the dress in hand. She held out the length of it so the woman could admire its beauty.

It was the last she had of Aengus.

"Only three pounds," my sister offers. "For a ticket to America."

The Tinker Woman says they have no money.

We don't believe her.

She goes into the brightly painted wagon and returns with a mysterious piece of paper. We study it, curiously.

"This, I found. It is a ticket to America."

"Where did you find it?" Roisin dares.

The woman tells us with clear eyes that she found it on the road.

"It is as stolen as my dress!"

The woman shakes her head. She found it in the pocket of a woman who could not use it anymore.

"You stole from the dead." Roisin is frightened. "May God forgive you. It may carry the fever."

The Tinker Woman looks at me, wondering if I have the fever. I smile at her and she smiles back.

"I want the ticket. I'll trade for it."

"That is a dead woman's ticket," Roisin warns.

"Whoever she was, I'll go in her place."

That night my sisters sat around the Tinkers' fire and ate stew from tin bowls. The Tinker Woman inspected me for signs of hunger, and saw that I did not need to eat.

She told my sisters to eat slowly or their stomachs would ache. I watched Roisin Dubh and Granya spoon their stew slowly into their mouths.

I love my sisters so much I promise St. Brigid I will never eat again if I can only stay with them.

Let my heart be your holy well.

Over our heads the stars burst into beautiful fires and fall.

13

I woke next to **Little Mary in the straw** of our high bunk in the Workhouse. A tiny, high window illuminated my sister's face.

It was the strange, dusky color our father's turned when he went to his bed and stayed there until he died.

I was more afraid than I had ever been. I had been off, on the road, and now my little sister was sick.

I pulled up Little Mary's nightdress and saw it: the rash on her shoulders and belly. She shook violently with cold, so I covered her again.

I piled all of our straw over her, and willed her not to die.

I blamed myself. I was always spying. I had left her alone when she needed me. I could never be where I was.

I scratched my legs, where fleabites worried me like the devil. My little sister shook more violently.

I climbed down the ladder and went running in my night-dress to find the Matrons.

Little Mary died as I was running through the hall.

VICTORIA TESTER

I lay on my back that night on a large scoured table in the huge, empty dining room. I had tried to stop the matrons, but they had taken my little sister's body away.

Laid it in a cart, to be placed in a common grave in the morning.

I could not remember my name. If I was Little Mary, or she, Una.

It didn't matter. It was I who laid in the cart, stiff and black and alone, and it was someone else who whispered the history lesson of our Schoolteacher.

He had gone to Dublin, we had heard, to stop the Irish ships that were carrying Ireland's cattle and wheat to England, and he had been hung, with twelve others.

But the Schoolteacher's face wasn't blue and his eyes did not roll onto his cheeks. He was still handsome, even without his golden chestplate. I ask him if he is an Angel.

"Has Ireland any claim to antiquity?"

"Yes," I whisper. "Her claim to antiquity is better founded than any other nation, other than the Jews or the Egyptians. No nation of the globe can trace such instances of early civilization. None possesses such proofs of its origin, lineage or duration of government."

"But is not Ireland's ancient history blended with fable?"

"This cannot be denied. But the early records of every nation, except those of the Jews, are blended with fable."

No one had to tell me later.

Rosin's hands were muddied from work in the thawing lazy beds.

Horses were lucky. I hoped maybe a horse could trample our field and make it sprout, even without seed potatoes.

Granya's hair was combed for her long journey.

98

My sisters faced each other in the doorway of the cottage.

It was time for Granya to depart.

A wagon approached in the distance, holding the others who were also bound for America.

"I will not let you perish here."

"Cross the ocean with your dead woman's ticket. I have no sister."

The wagon draws closer. Roisin Dubh turns away from Granya.

Granya touched our dark sister's rigid shoulder, but Roisin Dubh, icy with grief, gave no sign of farewell. They say ice and not blood ran in my dark sister's veins after Granya went away.

The wagon stopped, waiting.

Granya ran. She would send a letter through Father Brennan as soon as she reached America. She would pray that God would help us all until then.

She was already shaking with cold, and by the time she reached the port I knew she had forgotten the way back to our village.

I cried for two days because the magic box had never recorded Granya's face.

Roisin, her face severe, walked the path to the tiny church in search of Father Brennan. She opened the church door and found the nave empty.

"Father Brennan?"

Silence.

Roisin walked to where a picture of Mother Mary hung on the plaster wall. With a reverent hand she traced the features of Our Lady.

Then regained her severe look.

She knocked on the door of the little room that adjoined the nave of the church.

"Father Brennan?"

There was no answer. My sister opened the door cautiously.

Saw Father Brennan sitting black and rigid, quill and paper in hand. He had died of road fever in the act of writing one more letter to Your Honors.

I was mortified when I knew the priest had died.

I was sorry I had spied on him in his fragile humanity.

That I had left his books opened to passages he mistook for messages from the Holy Spirit.

Had stolen leftover potato skins that might have nourished him.

I was ashamed that I had, in my fear, and my love of running away fast, often blown out his candles.

I had even stolen his swan's quill, and kept it hidden under my straw mattress when I wasn't secretly practicing writing on oak leaves.

Worst of all, I had believed my own eyes and not the priest when he had shouted the men of our village were not starving wolves.

I had betrayed my village, and the very word of God.

Father Brennan had done his best for us.

Now he was dead, maybe for good. I wept inconsolably.

No one spoke of his return.

I found the black box.

It was laying in the grass beside a strange, solitary road that went to nowhere.

Somehow the English Photographer had mistaken the road, and now he sat at the green place where it ended. His boots, I saw, were gone from his feet, and now he went barefoot, as I did.

I could smell salt in the air and hear the wild sea. I could hear the hungry cries of gulls I knew were feeding on dead bodies.

I wanted the English Photographer to rise to his bare feet and pick up the black box.

To keep walking, even on this road to nowhere.

"Get up, Englishman."

Instead, he was wild. Panting with rage and shame.

He opened the carpet bag that held the glass world he was making and poured the mirrors of starving Ireland into the grass around us.

I looked at the fragile pieces as they reflected the grass.

I saw myself, reversed, my hair long and dark, in many of the mirrors, and I realized, startled, that the English Photographer had seen me after all.

He knows I am here.

But now he was breaking the glass world and the shards were cutting his hands.

He was destroying the Ireland he made with his reflections. There was blood on his hands.

I saw it, and was afraid.

He was not talking to Mary.

He was talking to himself, or maybe to the black box.

"Is looking an act of love? Should we be proud of that love? Looking saves nothing," he shouts. "Loving saves nothing."

He shouted that the glass worlds come between us to protect ourselves. "They separate us. They don't help us love."

The Photographer sat in the broken glass world, crying because he wanted to love. I was crying, too.

I was sorry because he had broken the world and I was sorry his cut hands were bleeding and his fine boots were gone.

He was silent for a long time.

I listened to the gulls fight.

They screamed, and the English Photographer and I were pierced through with regret.

He stood, walking barefoot among the sharp, shattered world, staring at its ruins.

His hands shook as he tried, tenderly, to reassemble the pieces.

His blood stained the images.

He talks to Mary again, but in a way that frightens me.

He will set Mary together, he promises, like that first morning in the garden. Her body was light and the light was so beautiful. He will set it back together. The world is breathing. It is good, it is good. He will bring her body into light.

His face burned with a strange happiness. Snow began to fall.

It is snowing on the magic black box and the English Photographer is delighted.

I realize the glass world of Ireland has broken his mind.

Maybe he will never leave it. Never go back to Mary.

I wrapped my shawl around his shoulders, and sat next to him for a long time. Then I remember: I must go home.

Through the frosted pane I saw the Farmer, his wife and their children at their long table, eating bacon, bread and potatoes. "Wheat prices will be higher in the fall," the Farmer told his wife. He will plant twelve more acres of it and they will live very well when it's sold.

His wife asked where, by St. Brigid's mantle, they would get another twelve acres.

The Farmer told her he offered the sum of the tenant's back rent to his Lordship if he'd sell the land to him, and his Lordship had agreed.

The Farmer's Wife froze. "The tenants will be turned out in the dead of winter."

I watched the Farmer shovel more bacon and potatoes into his gob.

The Farmer's children stopped eating.

The Farmer's Wife spoke as if she were waking from a dream.

When the Farmer first came to this farm with his father, she looked at his strong back and agreed to the match.

Her excuse was that her own gray father was getting too weak to work the land, but the truth was it was her wanting to roll in that bed with him.

What the Farmer's Wife knew now was what her father told her then. The boy with the strong back only looked like a man.

He was no man at all.

The woman stood and left her full plate on the table. The Farmer and his worried children went back to their meal.

Then the youngest child saw my face and cried out that the Hunger Fairy had come back and she was at the window.

14

I walked home in my nightdress. Even from the road I saw that our cottage still stood, and that Roisin Dubh stirred the soil of our lazy beds with a long stick.

It was too early for spring planting and there was not a single seed potato in what remained of our half-tumbled village. My sister worked the field anyway, alone.

I looked for blue smoke rising from Old Brigid's chimney, a sign that she lived, and was relieved when I saw it curling like the tail of my white cat, who ran to greet me.

Roisin watched, astonished, as I approached. She gasped at my shaven head.

She was speechless, not sure if I was a ghost. Maybe I had died in the Workhouse and walked home. So I threw my arms around her, and that made her furious.

"What will I feed you?"

"I'll eat grass."

"You ran away from the workhouse. Home to a graveyard. I should beat you."

"You told us to look back. You told us if we forget our true home, we become no one."

"And Little Mary?"

I go deaf. I hand her the small bundle of nettles I picked on the long road home.

Roisin understands, then, that Little Mary is dead.

She holds me to her empty middle and rocks us both.

"Where is your hair?"

"I didn't need it anymore."

"Where is your shawl?"

"The English Photographer was colder than I was."

She sees where the broken glass has cut my bare feet and my hands. I am so tired I can't even scratch the fleabites on my swollen legs.

I fall asleep standing, there in Roisin Dubh's thin arms.

For once, no dreams waited for me. There was no one to run with. Nothing to follow.

When I woke, Roisin Dubh was not in the cottage.

She'd taken her shawl and gone out. I got out of bed. My legs were weak and I shook with cold, but I went up the wooded hill to look for my sister.

I found her there with Liam, and listened from the oaks.

"Those of us who are left are to be turned out. The Farmer will feather his nest with our misery."

Liam wanted to plant the Farmer under his stolen fields. The ancient lands of the O'Coffey's.

Roisin would not listen. The time of dreaming was over. It was time to live.

Liam dreamed anyway. He remembered when they were children. They wore spring oak leaves in their hair, and pretended to marry.

Roisin was bitter. "Once upon a time. 'Twas neither your time, nor my time, but somebody's time, there lived a girl and a boy."

The girl and the boy, I saw, were not dead.

"Come with me," Liam says. "We'll go on the road."

"Fever lives on the road."

"No, fever lives in the cottages, in the cities and the ships. On the road we would be free of the fever. Free of Landlords. We'd owe nothing."

Roisin would not leave Old Brigid.

"Whoever wants to go with us will go."

I'll go, too, I decide. And the white cat.

"Brigid is too old to go on the road."

"That old battle-axe will outlive the land itself. Tomorrow, she'll be a young girl again."

Hope struggles in my sister's hollow face.

Liam sees it. "We'll leave before the Farmer and the Bailiff arrive with their evictions."

"If only we had a cart."

I think of the English Photographer's cart. The brown horse with big eyes pulling it across Ireland.

"You'll be riding."

Roisin is puzzled. Then incredulous. "Not Roisin Dubh."

The true mare the Landlord called the Queen's Pride.

"I gave you that horse the day she was born."

"They'll hang you, you idiot!"

But Liam answers there are few men about the place now. The Landlord took his family to England when his youngest daughter, who looked like me but owned flying swans, died of fever.

Had they draped the mirrors in black silk so the poor little girl could not look back at us?

Now it was said that for the first time anyone could remember, people were bludgeoning the swans with rocks, wringing their long necks and carrying them home.

Dawn, Roisin lit our fire with a hurried, whispered litany.

Kindle in my heart the coals of love, Jesus, son of Mary, pure and bright, for my enemy, my family, my friends, for the wise, the unwise, the enslaved, from chance encounters with the lowest of things up to the highest of names.

I shake with cold, but I am filled with joy looking at my dark sister. I want to tell you I love you.

My teeth are chattering. Roisin pulls up my grass stained nightdress and sees the rash on my belly.

"No," I protest.

Liam taps on the cottage door, but Roisin goes deaf.

I don't want Liam to see me naked. He goes to the little window and peers through a crack in the shutter.

"Go away," my sister says. "Stay away until Una is better."

"I want to go home," I say.

Roisin goes back to the fire, and with strong breaths, she makes it blaze high.

Old Brigid walks through the cottage door as though it is not latched. She is the same ancient Brigid but now there are two of her.

One very young, one very old.

They are carrying a pail of milk. Then they see me.

Roisin tells both Brigids they must go. "It is road fever."

Now there are three Brigids and the third is very angry at the road.

Her breath makes the fire blaze even higher, and she looks down at me, into my hidden selves.

"No," I say. "The stolen swan feather is mine. I want to keep it."

When I wake again I'm in Brigid's cottage.

They've taken away my wild bird feather and faced my bed north and south, and they've tied me close to Niamh of the Golden Hair, the white cow.

The window of Brigid's cottage glowed with the strange light that comes before light.

I woke up again, too weak to move or speak. I don't open my eyes. My face felt swollen and my lips too thick to make words.

Old Brigid dozed in her chair. Roisin crouched near me, watching.

It is a dangerous time, just before dawn. Now, most departing souls choose to go.

I feel something soft, like an owl's wing, brush my face. Niamh does not like it, and swishes her tail. I do not know if I should stay or go. Roisin shooes the soft wing away.

Lays her own hand over me.

I open my eyes and my sister utters a cry of delight. She smooths my hair and holds my hand. I fall into a deep well and cannot climb out again to find her.

I heard Brigid when she woke and added more peat to the fire. They must not let the fire die, or it could weaken me.

She milked the cow next to my ear, crooning quietly. Give me the milk, my treasure, give me the milk, my treasure, give me the milk and thou shall have the blessing of the Queen of Heaven.

I hope she won't rub dung over Niamh's udders.

I slept.

I woke again and saw Roisin crumbling an ugly dried herb into a pot of boiling water. I wanted to protest but I couldn't.

Brigid came in, carrying a basket. It made me furious.

I know the basket is empty. No matter what it holds, it is empty.

It is fairy food, and if we eat it we can never go back home.

Brigid takes eggs from the basket, and a loaf of bread. I hear her bless the Farmer's Wife, but the empty basket fills me with rage.

Damn the Farmer's Wife, too. I hope her left ear is on fire.

I am as furious with the world as if it were the other, glass one.

I want to break it, too.

I rage against Roisin Dubh for readying a field that will never be planted with potatoes. I hate the earth that is always under her fingernails. I hate her stories, I hate her singing.

I spit on Granya on a ship frozen in the Atlantic, and on Michael who waited for his own Jailers. Who would not run away with me from the Landlord's elegant dining room.

I'm furious with Little Mary for staying behind in the mass grave at the Workhouse. For not climbing out and walking home at my side.

I'm furious with my father Conall for being dead, and for killing my mother, and with my dead mother for never visiting me.

Not even once, in a mirror, or a dream.

I hate Aengus for the chains on his legs and Barra for staining the snow red. I hate Liam and his false music for building a road to nowhere.

I hate the priest for writing his useless letters to Your Honors.

I despise Old Brigid for being old, and for believing the land will always be young again. I am angry with Niamh for giving us milk.

I am angry with the last wolf of Ireland, who did not run fast enough.

I am angry with the earth that betrayed us. With the English Queen who betrayed us. And with the very Mother of Heaven who does not lay her wing over us.

Maybe, Mary, too, is dead.

I cannot find the magic box, or the English Photographer.

The roads of my country where my spirit walks are made of broken glass. I teach myself to walk barefoot over shards.

The roads are lonely. There is no more grass. It has all been eaten by humans, and by the sheep that were brought to replace us.

Now our island is made of light and stone. There isn't a single grass blade left in Ireland.

"Where have you been?" a Black Dog growls, sneaking up behind me. "I have been following you for two years." He has seven red tongues and they are all hungry.

He tries to take me up the chimney but I refuse to go.

He wants to cut off my hand. "The hand of a dead child can work miracles," he laughs.

I scream. He tries to carry me on his back to Spain, where everyone knows the Dead live.

The Dog riddles me: "It ate everything that came, and everything that will, and still it never gets its fill."

I don't know, I don't want to know.

He turns himself to a Black Carriage drawn by Black Horses. The Carriage, I know, will never leave this earth empty.

It will fly to the cemetery.

I fall to my knees and hold to the dark earth.

It is Roisin Dubh. She stands up out of the field in a clean red dress, her black hair shining.

She throws a stone at the Black Dog who runs away yelping, his three tails between his legs.

"Stay here, Una. Stop running away," Roisin scolds.

She hauls me to my feet. "Don't be lazy. It's almost St. Padraig's Day. I should slap you. Who will help to sow the seed potatoes?"

15

I woke into a soundless world and found Brigid's cottage filled with brilliant light.

I got out of bed and walked over to a large table where my father Conall Mac Cormaic, alive and strong, was seated, his lit pipe fragrant between his teeth. He offers a clay pipe to the English Photographer who nods and lights it with sparks from his thumbs.

Roisin and Liam, now expecting their first child, sit to my father's right, smiling at me as I look at everyone in wonder. Roisin wears a neat red dress, and there is no earth under her fingernails.

Next to my oldest sister and her husband sit Granya and Aengus, now also married. Granya is wearing the stolen green dress and holding a small clay mug of whisky.

Next to my red-haired sister, my brother Michael sits, his dark hair brushed clean of oak leaves, and next to Michael is young Barra, with no sign of blood on his shirt, who smiles absently back at my stare.

There is also Father Brennan, who is listening patiently, his fingers still stained with ink from his quills, to Old Brigid, who, in her fine carved chair, looks stern in her story.

Then winks at me.

Next to her sits Little Mary, swinging her round legs against her stool as she scolds the fat Viking chickens that peck near the hearth for trying, as always, to set our Irish cottage on fire.

I take my place on the empty stool next to Little Mary. My white cat wraps himself around my legs.

There is joyous expectation on everyone's faces as they turn towards someone at the hearth.

I turn towards her, too.

It is a tall, smiling woman who is carrying a large, steaming bowl of potatoes towards us.

It is my mother.

She is with us.

This, I know now, is heaven.

I decide to stay.

The magic black box rests quietly in a corner. There is no need for a glass world.

Through the open doorway, field upon field of potato plants blossom, green and purple and glorious.

When I open my eyes I am still filled with the dream.

Now I know my invisible eye is better than the magic black box.

The black box had never let us spy on heaven. The glass world it gave us was easily lost or broken.

Now I loved and did not hate the invisible eye in my forehead.

It had punished me and it had made me different from others.

It had sent me on dangerous journeys.

But it had also shown me my mother's face.

It had shown me heaven.

Old Brigid is bending over me. Smiling in spite of herself: "Una lives."

Then she looks stern. "Sleep."
And I do.

Liam walked a hidden path towards our ruined village, a wild hare dead in his hand.

Then I smelled something good as the door closed and I saw Old Brigid carry a large bowl of stew, made from the hare, to Liam.

There, near the O'Coffey scalpeen, she moved away from him and stood at a distance to protect him from the fever. Liam ate gratefully, blessing Brigid's old hands.

Only then does he see the sorrow on her face.

He throws the empty bowl against the earth.

"They may live," Old Brigid tells him. "We must wait."

Now Liam is alone on the wooded hill. It isn't Liam.

He never threw the bowl against the earth. He is eating the hare stew, and Brigid is watching him intently.

It is and it isn't Brigid. Her nails are black with earth.

"I am not the old woman I seem. Kiss me, Liam O'Coffey, and they will live. The land will be green again."

Liam wants to throw the bowl of stew but he doesn't. He's hungry. He hesitates.

"I am young and handsome. I won't kiss an Old Hag."

Brigid is sorrowful. The roses in her ancient face sink, and the lines deepen.

"Too proud to kiss me? Then the land will stay barren."

Liam wakes in the forest. There is no wild hare. He throws his empty bowl hard against the earth and curses it.

We're cold with fear from our dark dream.

Old Brigid's strong breath keeps the fire blazing high.

"No," I hear myself say.

I want to feel Roisin's cool, wide hand against my forehead. I sleep.

I go looking for my dark sister who is nowhere to be found.

Old Brigid is sweeping the yard.

A neighbor woman, keeping a safe distance from the old woman's fever ridden cottage, calls out:

"God bless you. I've brought a soup bone. I'll leave it here."

She lays the bone on a clean stone.

"May God repay you," Brigid tells her. "How are your children?"

"I have two alive. We're going to walk to Dublin now we're being turned out. Come with us, Brigid."

"I am waiting for a guest."

"Is he someone important?"

"Yes," Brigid answers.

"What will you feed him?"

"I'll offer him nothing. He may take all I have."

It is Death Brigid is waiting for.

"Come to Dublin with us. Let your guest find nothing here."

"Someone must be here when he arrives," Brigid says.

The village woman shakes her head. "If I meet him on the road, I'll misdirect him and send him to London."

"May God protect you."

"A blessing does not fill a belly."

When I woke that night, Roisin Dubh, I saw, was still sleeping.

Brigid sat sleepless in her ornate chair in the firelight, watching over us.

The old storyteller had wanted to sell the chair, but for Brigid and Rosin and Granya together, they had found, it was too heavy to carry to town.

The window was gold with sunrise.

A speckled magpie, brought to Ireland by Cromwell's soldiers, sang on the windowsill.

Brigid threw a rag at it, to scare the bad luck away.

She blew on the fire and took her pail to go for water.

I saw what she saw at the river: a great flock of cranes filled the sky and then landed at the river's banks, a sign of returning spring.

My head ached.

Liam laid an armload of peat in front of the cottage door.

I laugh because he's so thin, but I'm too tired to open my eyes.

Liam stands in the yard and peers through Brigid's cottage window, where the magpie landed.

"They're alive still," I hear Old Brigid say.

"Kiss me, Brigid," Liam begs.

"You're losing your thin O'Coffey wits," she scolds. "Go away or you'll die yourself."

Liam hangs turnips in a bag on the end of a long branch. Sticks it through the open window. He takes the empty water pail and goes to fetch water from the river.

He must be going to watch the return of the cranes.

"It's unlucky to kill a crane," I warn Liam. But it is only the sunlight laughing at me.

I wake to firelight.

Brigid watches from her carved chair.

I can turn my head a little, and I see that Roisin is asleep in Brigid's straw bed.

Her face is a dusky hue and her lips are swollen. Her breath is torn.

"Roisin Dubh," I call. My little black rose.

I call and call.

It is not my voice.

It is a river of silence where I am calling my dark sister in the voice of the cranes.

16

oisin Dubh died of fever as I opened my eyes at dawn. The fire had become ashes. Brigid slept in her chair. The magic black box had not yet found our village, or my dark, humble sister.

No glass world would ever reflect the strong bones of her face, or her earth-stained hands. The world would say my Roisin Dubh did not exist. That she had no story.

I lay there late into the morning.

There was nothing.

I listened for the motion of any spirit except my own.

The birds began to sing.

I go to Old Brigid and try to rouse her. The old woman opens her eyes, but can do no more.

Niamh lows, and I open the cottage door to free her, flooding the room with light.

I follow Niamh of the Golden Hair into the yard in my nightdress.

She ambles away.

Liam is in the yard with a pail of water. When he sees me swaying there his hopes are kindled.

He goes past me into the cottage to see Roisin.

He finds her. Dead.

It was me who killed her, Liam. I brought the fever from the road.

He isn't Liam anymore.

He runs out.

I am the frail ghost who trails after him over the path to the Landlord's estate.

I watch him saddle Roisin Dubh, the true mare, as if to ride her away.

I don't want him to go, but he is not Liam.

We don't notice when a door opens in the back of the barn, and someone comes in.

I watch as Liam races Roisin Dubh through the open barn doors, and then, too late, I open my mouth as the Farmer steps forward in grim silence.

His rifle raised and aimed at the escaping O'Coffey.

The Farmer shoots him in the back.

Killing him.

I returned to Old Brigid's cottage.

Offered her water from the pail. She is very weak, but she drinks through swollen lips.

She tells me, harshly, to go away.

That I am not welcome here.

I act like I am deaf. I put more peat on the fire. I sit on the little stool next to Old Brigid, who no longer stirs.

I don't look at Roisin.

The birds are welcoming spring outside the window.

I call Granya.

I call her and she sits up from a dream in the hold of the coffin ship on her way to America, among a crowd of ragged, half-starved Irish who share her berth.

"Granya," I shout. She races from the steerage to the deck of the ship, where sailors are lowering the bodies of the dead into the sea.

She looks around, searching desperately.

Stops short at the sight of the water around her.

A dark young Irish woman without a shawl, earth under her nails, comes to Granya's side. "They call it a bowl of tears. I wish to God it were something stronger. What is your name?"

But Granya is cold. Her lips turn blue.

When she woke up she could not remember her name.

The woman tries, sister-like, to comfort her. "What do you remember?"

I shout my sister's name but she does not hear me.

She shivers with cold. Her hands burn red with cold.

"Surely," the dark young woman says, "you remember the Hunger."

Granya shakes her head as if the woman's words are ridiculous. Truly, she has never known a care except for this sudden cold that goes to her very bones.

"What do you remember?" the woman asks, sober.

Granya has forgotten us.

The stolen dress, and its thief who loved her. The precious pubic hair she gave him.

Even the dead woman's ticket.

"Only this sea. This big, big sea."

O, my Granya. My Grace of many graces. Mary's wing over you.

They say Gray Man chased you and sank your ship to the rolling bottom of the sea.

But you were not on it.

You walked to Dublin where you became a whore.

You were sold on an auction block to a rich family in Boston, where the man of the house crept to your narrow bed in the attic.

You were thrown, shamed by your belly, into the street.

You burned to death in a locked shirtwaist factory in New York.

You hoarded enough money to buy an ice cream parlor, a hat shop and a liquor store, and you never wore any dresses except silk, and green.

You went as a mail order bride to a German farm on the Iowa prairie where you were driven mad by loneliness and wind.

You died of syphilis.

You lost your womb and went onstage and wore magnificent hats.

You joined exiled Irish rebels and incited men to noble violence.

You drowned on the Erie Canal and you roasted in the Great Fire of San Francisco.

Your face went unblemished far into your old age.

You became a famous actress and married the prince of a small Catholic country, and you have not forgotten us.

O, my Granya.

I am still waiting for your letter.

It is a lie that someone always lives to tell the story.

I lay down. I will never get up again.

After a while, I open my eyes.

I rise.

I take Roisin Dubh's shawl and put it on.

I set my feet into her shoes. They are big.

I look inside a tied cloth bundle and find a loaf of bread.

I carry it with me.

I walk out of the cottage without looking back at the silent Roisin Dubh or Old Brigid.

The white cat follows.

The little white cat, white, white, white.

I close the door on my dead.

The English Photographer stands, rooted, in our empty potato field.

His face dark with road fever.

He approaches with the battered black box.

I know his mind is broken, but I want to be polite.

"Hello," I say, and I ask, "What strange thing do you carry?"

He doesn't speak Irish, but he understands me.

He tells me he doesn't know what the magic box is.

I don't speak English, but I understand him.

He can tell I am disappointed.

So he says that the magic box is magic because it changes anyone who looks through it.

Sometimes it gives them a disease called sorrow that nothing ever cures.

I want him to look at me through the battered box anyway.

He agrees, only to please me.

The white cat and I stand solemn and still so that we can exist in another fragile, glass world.

Will we be broken?

The Photographer says it is I who am looking. I who am seeing a sad, fat Englishman with a magical machine. He is thin, and very ill, but I say nothing.

I know why the English Photographer has come.

I know, now, why he has been in Ireland all along.

He has come all this way, leaving behind his own Mary, to trade places with me.

He has looked at me through the black box so I may live.

I thank him.

It is not my business and now, I know, it is time for me to live, and go.

I wave a polite good-bye. Walk towards the road away from my ruined village.

My panicked white cat runs after me.

The English Photographer abandons the black box in the yard.

He opens the door to Old Brigid's cottage.

Old Brigid stirs, as I know she will, and sees, with gratitude, that I am gone.

With a strict dignity she nods a stern welcome towards the Englishman.

"You are welcome. Bless you if you lock the door, Stranger."

The Photographer latches the door so they may both die.

Away from sorrowful or curious eyes.

Then he goes to the window and closes the shutters on Ireland.

Vanquishing all light.

I walk the Hunger Road.

It stretches and curves far into the heart of my country.

In the distance I watch the approach of the Tinkers' bright wagon.

You will say that I walked to Dublin, where I survive, to this day, in a tenement.

You will say I perished, mute, my ghost perennial as the hungry grass.

I went to Liverpool and then to America, where I became a Clairvoyant and a famous Photographer.

I never walked out of the cottage whose stone walls were tumbled over us.

I lived, and climbed into the Tinkers' wagon.

I became the great grandmother of a living spirit of the road.

You.

A Traveller child who ignores the angry horns of trucks and automobiles.

Who looks between the horse's ears. And laughs.

ACKNOWLEDGMENTS

Thank you first of all, Phillip, for your own strongly Irish heritage and your joy in Una Mac Cormaic and this little book, which were the cornerstone for its writing.

Thank you, Tom Hayden, for your collection *Irish Hunger: Personal Reflections on the Legacy of the Famine,* which haunted me into finding this story.

Thank you, Ann Veenstra, extraordinary therapist who restored my heart, mind, memory and ability to pray, after long months of Famine study.

Thank you, Diane Freund (1944-2010), marvelous literary angel whose fierce love and lively joy in both Una Mac Cormaic and myself kept, and yes, keep, my efforts going.

ABOUT THE AUTHOR

 Victoria Tester is a poet and dramatist whose first book *Miracles of Sainted Earth* (University of New Mexico Press 2002) won the Willa Cather Literary Award in Poetry and whose *New Mexico Ghost Play Cycle*, a chronology of fifteen plays of thirty women of southern New Mexico, includes stories of Irish, Scots, Welsh and Cornish miners and immigrants. Tester holds an M.A. in Creative Writing and Literature from the University of Houston's esteemed Creative Writing Program. She has taught literature and creative writing, worked as a photojournalist on the Mexico border, and is co-founder and coordinator of the San Isidro Bean Project serving hands-on entities working to address the humanitarian hunger crisis on the Mexico border. She is a novice in the Third Order Society of St. Francis.

Made in the USA
Monee, IL
30 October 2020

46421522R00080